VALKYRIE'S SIGHT

For Sheila Beatrice Hancock, the greatest storyteller I
will ever know.

Valkyrie's Sight

KATHERINE GINBEY

Contents

Chapter One

"All I'm saying is that if you kill yourself in a certain way, it won't even hurt. Then we could be the cutest ghost couple in this place." Brock told Val in a confident tone as he draped himself over the desk next to hers.

Not that it mattered as the person currently sitting at that desk couldn't see him. Only Val seemed to have that pleasure and if she didn't have eighteen years' worth of experience seeing grizzly ghost wounds, his gunshot to the chest would have put her off of pretty much everything.

Val raised her eyebrow as she sipped from her water bottle but said nothing. She had some slip-ups in the past and since it was just after the Christmas break of her senior year, she shouldn't care about doing it now, but no one liked being called a weirdo. She also knew that Brock was kidding. If he even thought she was thinking about hurting herself, he'd use whatever ghost powers he could think of to wrap her up in a protective bubble until her parents got home.

As was the case with idiotic boys, Brock was also drop-dead gorgeous. He was a cliché nineties heartthrob before they became a cliché. Val could have cut herself on his jaw-line and his hair was gelled into a devil may care style. The only thing he was missing was a varsity jacket because, and it was a direct quote, 'Chicks dig artist types.'

Not that he hadn't been on the football team, he had, but he hadn't worn it around everywhere. Val was one hundred percent certain that he was only hitting on her because that was his natural state and all the other girls that could see him had watched him die through a classroom window before being massacred themselves.

"Come on, Valkyrie, talk to meeeeeee." Brock started swinging his legs back and forth. "Shoot me that pretty little smile at least. I'm dying over here- get it?"

Val's lips did twitch into a smile then as she focussed on her notebook and oh so slowly started writing the date in cursive on the top right corner of the top line. The class was slowly filling up around her and the living conversations filled out the one-way conversation. Val caught snippets of girls discussing what they did at new year's, boys discussing a new game that got released over the break and how the graphics were so 'janky.' The girls' conversation quickly became louder than the others and you only had to listen for two seconds to realise it was because they thought they were bragging.

"No, I'm serious, he heart-eyes reacted to my story! Look!"

Val didn't have to turn around or even glance behind her to recognise that southern drawl. Kimmy Blake had moved to the small town of Drayton, Massachusetts from Georgia the year after Val, but the pretty blonde hadn't had any trouble making friends that were equally gorgeous and skinny- including Holly Meers, who always gestured with her arms when she spoke and could be identified from the jangle of bracelets always on her wrists.

"Oh my god no!" Holly gasped. "He went like, viral over the break as well."

"250,000 followers isn't *viral*, Holly." Someone scoffed, and this time Val did turn to look, spinning in her seat slightly under the guise of a stretch. Ah. It was Barbie

Daniels that completed the trio. She was tall and ridiculously thin with smooth ebony skin. She always looked ready to walk a runway and Val supposed if your Instagram caption was going to be 'Nigerian Princess' and you're not Nigerian, then the princess part had to look real.

"It's better than your 3000 though, isn't it?" Holly responded coolly and Val noticed other students glancing at the trio as well. Brock had fully spun around to witness the action.

When pretty girls got into a catfight, people noticed, especially when the pretty girls were doing it over an even prettier boy. The boy they were discussing was obvious to everyone. Only one student in the school had such a large following and it was solely due to him being attractive and somewhat funny enough to get away with being a nerd. Even Val followed him on Instagram, and she used that as often as Brock had a pulse.

Like the devil, James Rogers always arrived when you were talking about him, and he breezed into the room smelling like cotton candy and looking just as delicious. He slid into place at a desk right next to the trio of girls and his friend he walked in with took the space in the middle, kissing Holly on his cheek as he passed.

Callum Sanders is an average looking boy with an average size brain. He was lab partners with one of Val's friends Jennifer and she was often stuck doing extra work for their assignments to keep her grade up. He was attached at the hip to Hollie- or rather, by the tongue.

Now that the very important students had arrived, Mr Hendricks decided to start the lesson. He started to scribble his lesson objectives on the smartboard and Brock leaned forward to the stage whisper in Val's ear that "If she started wearing shorter skirts, then pervy professors would wait for her to start class as well."

Val muttered a response of "Bite me" as she copied down the objectives. It didn't matter that she had spoken at a minuscule volume- Brock had heard and started to chuckle loud enough to drown out Mr Hendrick's welcome back speech.

It was a generic speech. None of the teachers at this school were particularly inspiring, although a few of the art teachers tried around exhibition season, which Val only knew was coming because Jennifer spent a worrying amount of time hidden away in the corner of the school's mediocre art studio to get ready.

"Now I know it's the first lesson back after winter break and we would all like to ease back into school nice and slow. But it's senior year and you don't always get what you want." Mr Hendricks declared as he propped himself on the corner of the desk and crossed his arms. Brock remarked that he clearly thought of himself as Robin Williams. Val was pretty sure he had never watched Dead Poets Society and was just going off of a vague reference he once heard.

"But what you are getting is paired up for a month-long project about Shakespeare adaptations. Pick one as a pair and analyse it. You can choose the format. An essay, a video or PowerPoint. I'll put the requirements for each up on the board as you pair up and *no*, Miss Daniels, you will not get to pick those pairs." Mr Hendricks slid a piece of paper out of his tray with a dramatic swish. Brock gave a snort that caused Val to smile.

Mr Hendricks started to read out the pairs and, in true teacher fashion, he had separated pretty much everyone from whom they had chosen to sit next to. Since Val picked a random seat near-random people, her partner was pretty inconsequential to her. Brock started bragging that she would technically be in a group of four and Jess was awesome at English back in the day when they were studying it so-

"Valkyrie Ellis and James Rogers." Mr Hendricks cut off the ghosts hyping up speech and Val snapped her head up to make sure she heard that correctly. That was a particularly vengeful move on Mr Hendrick's part and Val heard a mixture between a snort and a laugh from behind her. It was quickly cut off and Val heard the sound of a chair scraping against the cheap linoleum floor.

"He's coming over," Brock told her, suddenly in front of her desk and blocking her view of the board. "Running his hands through his hair as well like a total wet wipe." Val shot him a slight glare, but Brock carried on. "He must have really got under Mr Hendrick's skin to get put with you. No offence, gorgeous."

Val only took slight offence, especially since the reason most people avoided her was that she looked at and responded to invisible beings. Other than that, she was at least averagely pretty (Claire was particularly brutal about her looks whenever she deigned to talk to her) and she aced all her classes (although she did remind herself that the ghosts gave her the answers if she wasn't sure) and she had gotten her anger about it all out before they moved here just before her Sophomore year. She wasn't a *catch*, but she wasn't exactly pariah material.

"Hi." James greeted them once he got to her desk. Everyone in the class was shuffling or had already shuffled to their new spots and James reached through Brock, spun the chair from the desk in front of her round and sat himself down on it. Brock gave a massive shudder and then glared at the back of the other boy's head as if he suddenly had laser vision and could burn through it.

"Hi." Val breathed and tilted her head to the side to catch sight of the board. "So, I'm happy with any format," Val admitted as she delved right into it.

"Oh, I'm good, how are you? Yeah, I'm excited to work with you too!" James told her as he pulled out his notebook. Val's breath caught in her throat, and she went to snap back at him but then he looked up at her, smiling with a twinkle in his eye and Val realised he had been making a joke. Maybe he wasn't moderately funny after all. "I'm partial to the video format myself." James added, "I'm pretty good at editing and we could use clips. It'll make sure we hit the minimum time mark and teenagers are all about visuals."

Val blinked at him for a second and pressed her lips together as she thought about it. Her major points could easily be made into a voice-over and he wasn't lying. From the videos she had seen on his social media, he *was* decent enough at editing. "Video it is." Val agreed. "I was thinking for the adaption we pick something not as obvious. Every-one's probably gonna go for *Romeo and Juliet* or *Hamlet* but *10 Things I Hate About You* is a Shakespeare adaption and it's really easy to talk about."

"I'm glad I'm partnered up with someone that's got some brain cells." James chuckled. "But I've, um, actually never seen that movie. I've heard of it, but I never actually got round to it."

"Oh," Val blinked. "Um, I think you can stream it maybe? Or I have the DVD if you wanted to borrow it. If that's easier for you." Val realised she was speaking in tiny sentences every time she spoke to him and she must sound like an idiot. Her eyes flickered as Brock started moving around the room to eavesdrop on other projects and when she looked back, James was just staring at her, completely unbothered at being caught.

"We should watch it together," James told her, although Val hadn't been sure it was an option. She had already decided she would watch whatever they picked tonight with Chinese food and an empty house. "That is unless you have any massive objections to that idea."

"I was planning on watching it tonight while my parents are at work," Val admitted quickly because the objection of *I live at a halfway house for ghosts* isn't something normal people said to cute boys.

"Sooooo do your parents have a no boys over rule?" James asked with an eyebrow raise.

"Do NOT invite him over tonight." Brock hissed into Val's ear suddenly. "I'm serious. I'll go all poltergeist the second he puts a single toe on the property!"

Val covered her mouth and coughed twice. It wasn't a subtle signal, but it was effective, and Brock simply gave a huff as he moved a step or so backwards away from her. "I'm gonna go find Jess. She'll stop this." Brock decided in a mutter and before Val could even blink, the ghost was completely out of sight.

Val realised she hadn't answered and quickly told him, "Well no. But I doubt you're free on only a few hours' notice and you don't know me. I could be completely psycho like everyone says I am, and you'd be all alone with me in a house you've never been to."

"If you do kill me, I'll make sure my ghost tells someone it was my pretty English partner that did it." James shot back immediately. "I just thought it would be easier to create a project if we are, ya know, working together."

James's eyes had that playful twinkle in them again and without Brock here to loudly be her conscience, Val was blurting out a "Fine" before it even properly registered that he called her pretty.

James face split into a grin. "Great! I'll add you on Facebook after class and you can send me your address. I'll even bring some study snacks. You're not allergic to anything, are you?"

James was now babbling, and he had the kind of smile you automatically responded to. At least that was the excuse Val told herself as she grinned back at him.

"Actually, I was gonna order Chinese- wait. You're not scared of dogs are you?" Val asked, tapping her pen against the desk as she realised that would be an easy out for this weird turn of events.

"Love dogs!" James exclaimed as he leaned forward in his chair and crossed his arms on the top of its back. Val felt like she was being examined or at the very least judged as he continued. "What type have you got?"

"German Shepard. He's only three." Val would usually have taken out her phone and shown her lock screen, which was of Oz dressed up in a cute plaid bandana, but Mr Hendricks had started to wander around the classroom, and he was very confiscation happy.

"Cute. Big dogs are the best. So, you got him just after you moved here?" James tilted his head at her, and Val raised her eyebrows. She knew most of the students in her year at school had been in the same classes since they were learning to walk and talk, but the fact James remembered exactly how long ago she had moved here was a little weird.

It wasn't a small enough town to notice when every single new person moved in.

"Um yeah actually. Oz was a present from my parents as a kind of sorry for uprooting you thing," Val told him softly, pen tapping ceasing as she stared at him. "Without sounding like a pick-me girl, I didn't realise you paid enough attention to me to remember how long I've been here."

"You made quite an impression." James shrugged as if his attention was no big deal to anybody. He looked down at his notebook and started to doodle in the corners. "It's a small town. A new heart surgeon and a detective transfer over from a city as big as Chicago with a cute teenage daughter? Your family were basically front-page news as soon as you guys bought the house. Well...if the PTA had a newspaper that is." James kept his eyes focussed on his drawing. He didn't even glance up at her when he complimented her.

"I suppose I'm flattered. I'm also gonna ignore the fact you know my parent's jobs and that they bought the house." Val looked around the room, leaning back and crossing her arms in a mirror of James' earlier pose.

She thought she was looking quite nonchalantly out the windows and by everyone's desks as she waited for her friends to pop back into existence. It didn't usually take Brock that long to find Jess and frankly she could very much use the invisible wannabe prom queen whispering what to do in her ear.

"Hollie's mum was the realtor. She was quite proud that her mum managed to sell 'the big house' with only a video viewing. It meant she got a Gucci purse." James did glance up then and shot her a brief smile before returning to his drawing. "Apparently the house had sat empty for a while and was quite out of budget for her normal clients."

"Your memory about my house is weirdly good. Are you sure you're not just coming over to rob me?" Val joked, although she was serious about the first part. The mention of budgets made her squirm slightly. She hated talking about money but that was probably because she was very aware her family had it.

Her father also had Val's 'special gift' and had gone to medical school in Chicago. He used his loans to gamble with an unfair advantage of bookie ghosts in his ear, invested wins with the advice from a long-dead financial advisor and rounded it all off by becoming a highly qualified and sought-after brain surgeon with the advice from multiple ghosts in that field to guide him. Her mother was normal but driven and had become a cop and then a detective as soon as she was physically old enough and qualified enough to be.

"Oh, I'm very sure you could stop me if I was." James laughed properly then. "Although I would be tempted to dog-nap."

"The softie would probably go with you willingly as long as you kept stroking him all the way to the car." Val snorted and then almost swallowed her tongue as the ghost of Jess Poole was suddenly examining James' face, up close and personal like he was a priceless painting. Jess shot her friend a cheeky wink before slowly moving round to James' other side.

Jess was an incredibly pretty girl in a carefully coordinated outfit that was sadly ruined by the blood seeping out of the gunshot hole in the side of her neck. She was a case of wrong place at the wrong time and, in the school shooter's confession in his own last few minutes on the earth, was described as just 'collateral damage.' Val didn't think that had been any comfort to her parents.

Her mother had been incredibly brave during the whole thing, Val had found out. Her and Jess's father had split up and he had taken Jess's two little brothers with him when he left. She had gone from the women whose marriage all the racist little grandmothers gossiped about ("her husband's *black*, you know") to those same women discussing her tragedy with sombre faces ("Such a shame. She was a pretty girl even with her... complexion").

"Sounds like a plan to me. I mean, my mother would freak out because she thinks dogs are incredibly dirty creatures but I'm sure I could hide him in my room long enough to prove her wrong." James smirked at her, and Val playfully rolled her eyes at him.

"It's weird he brought up his mother," Brock called from where he had perched himself on the desk to the side of them.

"It's sweet he brought up his mother." Jess corrected before slowly nodding and backing away from James as if he had passed her examination, whatever that meant in her 90's teenage brain.

"Well, I promise my house isn't dirty." Val resisted the urge to roll her eyes again, but this time at the ghosts that had started bickering about if this was 'A good idea or not.'As if their decision was going to magically change Mr Hendrick's mind and have them moved into different pairs. Val glanced down at her watch.

Time had passed quickly, but then again Mr Hendricks had given his welcome back spiel, paired them up, pairs had got together and...actually, that didn't take that long. Most of the time had been spent talking to James, who seemed a lot more human in person than the ridiculously out of everyone's league mega hottie he was online.

He was a lot more approachable and the aura that most influencers seemed to have depleted to just basic human confidence. It made Val wonder what the hell social media had done to everyone's brains that she had ever viewed him as something different.

"So, Valkyrie, expect multiple DMs from me by the time you get to your next class. One of them will be asking for a dog picture," James joked as he started to put his notebook away. Val caught a flash of the doodle inside before it closed. It was good. Nothing spectacular but a very decent ensemble of cartoons. She had never seen any of that stuff on his socials.

"It's Val," she corrected quickly as she started to pack up as well. "Only my mother calls me Valkyrie and only if I'm doing something she would have to arrest me for."

James threw his head back and laughed. "So, you have a really cool, weird name that you don't want me to use? Oh, that's gonna cost you. Let's go with.....at least two dog pictures." James wiggled his eyebrows at her, and Val laughed back.

"Oh please," Brock snapped as he pushed himself to his feet. "Is this what he calls flirting? If we were back in my senior year, this dude wouldn't have a chance with anybody."

"This dude would have had a chance with anybody he wanted." Jess snorted. "He's totally hunky and funny but not broody. Val, you have to make out with him or I'm literally gonna die."

"Two dog pics it is." Val agreed loudly as she stood from her seat. "And my name is not cool: it is a gross injustice. You ever tried to find Valkyrie on a keychain?" Val jangled the nameless keychain she had on her bag zipper for emphasis. "Now with a name like James, I would be set for keychain life."

"You would also get confused with every other James in town. There are at least twelve in just this school. I've checked," James argued. "But there's only one Valkyrie Ellis." James dared to shoot her a wink after that, leaving without a goodbye.

Val had hit her thigh against her desk at that and she quickly ducked her head and headed towards the door as she heard Brock chuckle at her. She suddenly had an evening to plan for and the 'surprise' pop quiz that Miss Simmons had every first day back to go to.

Chapter Two

Jess tried to convince Val to change into something cuter for the 'study date,' but Val thought that was weird and he would notice, and it wasn't a date anyway: it was forced communication in a private setting. Brock had rolled his eyes and called her an idiot but wholeheartedly agreed that this was not a date.

James had messaged her and sent her a friend request all before she reached the end of the hall. She had sent him the two dogs' pictures a few minutes later (Jess kept telling her she didn't want to seem too keen cause that's how girls get bad reputations) but it was only the latest two from her camera roll.

James had still reacted with multiple love hearts and an *'oh he's gorgeous. What a good boy.'* The conversation had carried on throughout the rest of the school day with random large gaps on either side whenever class intervened, and Val was already more comfortable about the idea of him coming over.

Brock and Jess had promised to stay upstairs and away from the studying, so they didn't distract Val. Brock got a kick out of making Val react in public spaces and watching those around her try and figure out why and since he was initially against this arrangement, Val wasn't going to risk him even being on the same floor.

So, for the first time in a long time, Val was sitting in a ghost-free living room. Oz was curled up next to her on the couch on top of his dog blanket that was left on a specific cushion for him. He seemed almost bored by just Val's company, continuously moving his head to look around the room at the bookcase and armchair to try and find anyone extra. Jess in particular loved to curl up in it and chat.

Val's phone started to buzz as she was mid food order. The town had minimal options for takeout but the options that they did have were decent quality for how cheap it all was. The one expensive option that the town had was always solidly booked out at least two weeks in advance with everyone's anniversaries and proposals. Val's parents always chose to drive the extra hour into Boston whenever they got around to planning some alone time.

It wasn't a phone call but a video call and James' profile picture, all tousled hair and a large paperwhite grin, caused her to quickly run her hands through her raven black hair into something vaguely tidy before clicking an answer button.

"Hey. I've just grabbed some stuff and should be at yours in like 5?" James wasn't looking at her, his phone propped into place on his dashboard. Val could see a small section of the steering wheel and that James was focusing on the road.

"Okay, awesome." Val licked her lips. "I was actually about to message you. I'm getting some China dragon and was wondering what you wanted."

"Oh, you're spoiling me." James teased, and the screen froze for a half-second. When it jumped forward he was smiling. "I eat anything from that place. If it's got noodles, even better."

"Anything with noodles. Got it. If you get lost, then lemme know." Val told him before hanging up. That felt like a good last sentence, although if he got lost down this street then she was seriously going to worry about the outcome of the project.

Val lived down a clearly marked wide road with lines of large houses down either side. The road came to a dead-end at a large field with an enormous children's playpark taking up roughly half of the green space. Whoever had designed this part of town clearly expected multiple households to have multiple children.

The smallest house in the street was a four-bedroom but they had forgotten the fact that the only people who could afford them were older couples with grown-up children, if they had any at all.

They had all been pretty career-focused: had to be to save up enough to buy a house in such a nice area so close to Boston. Every house also had a pool in the back, as Val had found out the summer she moved here when every single neighbour had invited them over for a BBQ. The Ellis family had attended every single one and every single time, Val was the youngest one there.

The only times when people vaguely in her age range were there were during school holidays when the grand-children arrived, college boys and girls or pre-schoolers who only ever wanted to play hide and seek. Still- it was beautiful suburban America and if it hadn't of been for the ghosts, Val would have run all the way back to the gritty Chicago city centre.

Val finished up the food order, clicking the recommended noodle dish before she could spend too long panicking over if she had picked the right one and adding a bunch of basic sides like spring rolls to be a few more inches on the safe side.

Oz's ears pricked up and he was racing towards the door. Val pushed herself to her feet, straightened out her long sleeve and headed after him. She reached the door just as the doorbell rang and when she opened it, James was standing there with an overflowing paper bag and his eyebrows raised. The confused look quickly left his face and was replaced by a massive grin. James immediately crouched down to Oz's level, but the dog simply sat and stared at him.

At this lacklustre response, James tilted his head up to look at Val. "He's very well trained." Val chuckled. "You'll get a proper greeting once you're inside and not holding anything."

"That is well trained," James admitted as he hopped back up to his feet and took a dramatic step inside. Val quickly scrambled back a step to create a little difference. "I got sodas and some fizzy candy and then I thought you might prefer chocolate so there's some of that in there too. Oh, and popcorn, because you can't watch a movie without popcorn." James ran his free hand through his hair and Val suddenly wished she had Jess suddenly appearing to confirm to her that James seemed a little nervous.

Val smiled at him and held her arms out for the bag. "I'll take that if you want and then you can get your proper welcome from who you actually came to see."

James laughed but handed her the bag, and the second it was firmly in Val's hands, Oz jumped up onto his hind legs and his front paws were on James' shoulders. Oz was a big dog and even though James was easily six feet tall, the two were nose to nose almost.

James started to coo that Oz was such a gorgeous, behaved boy, running his hands through Oz's fur and ruffling his ears as Val headed into the living room and placed the bag onto to glass tabletop.

It was a few minutes before Oz trotted back into the living room and onto his spot on the couch and James was hot on his heels. The teenager was looking around him as he went, and Val was quickly glancing around to try and find if there was something embarrassing she should have hidden before he got here.

Family photos were displayed in frames all across the walls, mixed in with certificates, diplomas, awards, and crayon drawings made by Val and the children involved in her mother's cases or her father's patients. Children often gifted them hand-drawn things and they kept it all, most up in the attic in protected boxes.

The ones that made the wall were the particularly hard or emotional ones. Pride of place out of this collection was the hand-drawn card from Valkyrie Patrick's little sister. It was the case that brought her parents together and where they had picked Val's name.

The drawing was atrocious and if it wasn't for the children's scrawl underneath you would never have known it was supposed to be a stickman doctor, but it had been made by a traumatised three-year-old and had been her mother's excuse to go see her father again, so it had been on the living room wall in every place they had ever lived, even before Val was so much as the thought of.

"Cool décor," James told her nonchalantly as he stopped to stare at one particular photo. All the frames were the same, classic black on a light grey wall. The house's entire colour scheme was grey, black, and white. White was mostly in the kitchen and the bathrooms, a scattering of accessories here and there. "You're close with your folks huh?" The picture he was staring at was a selfie of the trio with big ben in the background.

"I guess so." Val shrugged because what teenage girl admits her parents are some of her best (living) friends? "That was on my dad's fortieth. Mum surprised him with a week away in England. He loves everything British."

James turned his head to look at her and slowly grinned. "Well that explains that I guess." James waved his hand in a gesture to the ornament on top of the bookshelf in the corner.

It was a gorgeous metal sculpture of the London skyline. It had been Val's gift to him that very same birthday. The opening gift to the main one in a way as he had been given that first and as he was gushing over it told he would have to compare it to the real one. Val's dad always told them it was the best birthday ever.

"I got that at a flea market back in Chicago. The dude was selling it for like five bucks along with loads of other junk. He just wanted some stuff out of his house." Val rambled, fumbling the corners of her shirt with her thumbs. Her phone screen flared up and Val checked it quickly. "Food's on its way. I got you a chow mein because you said you liked noodles and there's loads of sides 'cause I'm kinda picky."

"Awesome thanks. Text me your details and I'll send you my half." James told her as he moved around the table and took a seat. Since Oz and his blanket were settled on half of the couch and Val against the armrest, it left him no choice but the middle of the couch in-between them. Val quickly moved her legs out of the way and reached for her notebook and the remote.

"Don't worry about it." Val shrugged as she skipped through to a fresh page. She neatly scrawled *10 things notes* before she realised that James has simply opened up the notes section on his phone and was watching her.

"I'm old school," she explained lamely although James hadn't said anything. "Did you wanna start it now or eat first or..." Val wasn't exactly sure what another option would have been.

"Food first sounds good. Won't miss anything that way and I get the feeling you get hyper-focused on stuff." James locked his phone and slid it upside down onto the table. "I realised I probably freaked you out a little bit earlier knowing so much about your house, so thanks for actually letting me in. I promise no thieving or murdering." James made a gesture over his heart. "Scout's honour."

"Well, I'm sure many murdering thieves have never broken scout's honour." Val's smirked over at him. "But thanks."

"You get any questions about my house to make it even? I'll tell you all about my haunted toaster or the squeaky doorknob to the bathroom. Thrilling stories, I promise you." James started to absentmindedly stroke Oz as he looked at Val.

"I'm good. If I wanted to gather some info on you, I'd just load up your socials." Val reached forward for a soda can and popped it open with one hand as James chortled.

"Yeah, that sounds about right from a girl whose last Instagram post was from Halloween. Cute costume by the way. Ya don't see a lot of eighteen-year-old girls as X-wing pilots."

"I graduated Pilot school early," Val quipped as she realised that he was right.

She hadn't posted since October, not even the family shots from her visit to her grandparents for Christmas break or the small New Year's party her friends had held. She also realised that him knowing that meant he had gone looking. It crossed her mind that it was to make fun of her- his friends certainly liked to, but the way he was staring at her was different. The glint in his eyes was less malicious and more curious. Just as their eyes locked, the doorbell rang and both Oz and Val were up from their seats in seconds.

Val had already tipped on the app and took the food quickly with a smile and a polite chuckle at the horrendous joke made about Oz being 'Just a puppy then, eh.'

By the time she had ducked back into the living room, James had already cleared off the table, placing the notebooks and the bags of sweets onto the underneath shelf of it.

"I would have got plates, but I didn't wanna just go looking- "James began.

"I'll get 'em," Val told him as she gently dropped the bag of food onto the glass. James silently started to unpack the containers.

Val grabbed two glasses, two big plates and some forks just in case, juggling them back to the living room with Oz twisting around her ankles. Most dogs would have stayed with the food but Oz, with his ghost-seeing eyes and almost human-like brain, understood that the more he buttered up Val, the more likely he was to get a spring roll.

Val slid the plates into the gaps James had left and couldn't help but smile at how he had organised it all. The sides were placed in a horizontal row that created a sort of barricade between the two spots with each of their mains up at the top. It was incredibly aesthetically pleasing and going to be practical when it came to sharing stuff, but James almost looked ashamed to have been caught doing it. Val caught sight of his phone on the sofa next to him, the camera still open as he had quickly dropped it when she was coming in.

Val felt bad for her little dig earlier and handed him a fork. "Your Instagram's really good, ya know. I'm just not that...coordinated. Creatively I mean. I wouldn't even know how to make my life look so fun and bright and put together, so I just don't. I didn't mean it to sound like I was judging you or anything."

James took the fork and smiled at her. "Thanks. I just post myself. My cousin once told me I could make anything fun if I thought of it as a game and I've spent the last twelve years racking up those XP points, I guess." James reached over, picked up a spring roll, and bit it in half. He chewed thoughtfully while looking at her. After swallowing, he added, "Did that sound cheesy? It felt cheesy."

Val opened her mouth to respond but a voice from behind her made a disgruntled noise and said acidly "Yes. Super gross and nerdy too."

Val fake coughed into her elbow to play off her lack of response, keeping her eyes up and focussed on the space just behind James' head as Claire Rickards strutted into view.

Claire had been a teenage catalogue model in the mid-nineties and even after she was shot six times in the chest, she would never let you forget it. She had been designing her prom queen posters with her brand-new headshots the afternoon of the shooting and Val wasn't entirely sure she hadn't asked him 'not the face' as it was happening.

She was the kind of girl that low rise jeans were made for, and it was just her luck that she had been killed in a pair that was perfectly paired with a cute green daisy-patterned crop top. It was more early noughties than late nineties outfit wise and Claire always boasted she had been ahead of her time. Frankly, if Val was tragically left as an eighteen-year-old ghost, she probably would have focussed on something else.

"This is super boring. Your idea of a date is tragic. Now get me Jess: she's not coming when I call," Claire demanded as she came to a stop right next to Oz. The dog tilted his head to look at her before turning back to the two living people with the food. He had never liked Claire and it had annoyed the model to no end when the family had first moved in.

Val took a deep breath and answered quickly, "Only a little cheesy but I liked it," before quickly stabbing at a piece of lemon chicken and shoving it in her mouth in an incredibly unflattering way.

"Very mature." Claire scowled at her crossing her arms and popping her lip. It was unnervingly like the pose Val's mother always did when waiting for an explanation. "I'm serious: go get her or I'm gonna start moving stuff."

Val stared straight down at her plate as she piled her main onto it followed by a few of each of the sides. James started doing the same and between those two there was a verbal silence. Claire was huffing at being ignored and her bluff being called, but she eventually just settled herself into a perch on the edge of the armchair. "Well, I guess I'll just wait here then, shall I, *Valkyrie.*" Claire sneered, and Val's only response was to snap her fortune cookie in half.

"Whatcha get?" James asked immediately as he stirred his noodles. Val glanced over at him and pulled out the little strip of paper. She never cared much for the fortunes of the lucky numbers on the other side. She just liked the actual cookie.

"The love of your life will appear unexpectedly." Val drawled, rolling her eyes as she put the little piece of paper on the table. She popped half of the cookie into her mouth just as Brock appeared next to Claire, grabbed her arm, and they both disappeared. Val was focused on that so almost missed it as James finished his comment- "Tell you when I'm arriving next time."

Val choked down the cookie and turned to face him. "Sorry I was- what did you say?"

James raised one eyebrow at her and slowly repeated, although a lot less confidently, "So I just won't tell you when I'm arriving next time." Val frowned slightly and then it clicked.

"Oh!" Val chuckled. "The fortune. You're making a joke. Right." Val picked up her fork again and pointed it at him with an awkward smile. "Very clever. Top marks," Val babbled as she was tempted to excuse herself and head upstairs to find out exactly where Brock had taken Claire and why Claire needed Jess right now anyway- but no, Val, no. This was a ghost-free study night. Her fingers flexed around the fork as she finished off her plate. Ghost stuff later, high school study date now.

"Do you always make it a joke when people hit on you?" James cocked his head to the side.

"Do you always hit on girls you get partnered up with?" Val shot back.

"Absolutely not." James defended immediately. "None of them were you."

Val rolled her eyes and laughed at that. "That was cheesy. I'm sure it works at all those hopping parties though."

"I think hopping parties only happened in the seventies. Now the kids call them little gatherings. Ya know, just in case only a few people turn up."

"Well, now I just feel bad for them." Val leant herself back against the cushions. "It must be so exhausting worrying about that sort of thing."

James copied Val's pose and his shoulder was now resting against hers. "You don't care about that kind of stuff? Everybody does. They pretend they don't, but they do you can see it with how they act at school. All nice to everyone unless they have a group of people behind them so they can be cruel."

Val shrugged but she didn't move her shoulder away afterwards. She put it right back against his so now their arms were touching. "I don't. I know if I had a party, then no one would come or if they did, it would be to make fun of it." Val playfully tapped his knee. "Get called a freak for long enough and you stop caring about what it means."

"I don't think you're a freak. I don't think anyone genuinely thinks you're a freak; it's just...high school, ya know?" James whispered to her as he looked at her and Val could have sworn he glanced down at her lips.

"I'm pretty freaky. I accept that." Val whispered back, and it was true. She could speak to ghosts and sometimes she slipped up and did it in public or zoned out and ended up watching what ghosts were doing rather than still living people.

They always did more interesting things anyway since they knew no one could see them. Val would rather watch a dead teenager jam out in the hallway to their favourite song on a ghostly Walkman than a living one hunch over and blend in with the crowd of students listening to the morning announcements.

"Well pretty freaky...I think we are gonna have a kick-ass assignment and it's going to kickstart an awesome friendship." James playfully tapped her knee right back. "Ya wanna start the movie now?"

Chapter Three

"Would you just believe me that you look super hot?" Jess huffed from her spot at the end of the bed as she watched Val spin around in front of the floor-length mirror for the hundredth time that morning. Jess had picked out Val's outfit for the day, a black mini skirt and tee that had a sarcastic phrase embroidered delicately across the chest.

"Yeah, you're total bacon right now." Brock piped up as he laid just behind Jess on the bed, lazily throwing a stress ball repeatedly up in the air and catching it. Both girls turned to look at him with confused looks and he sighed as he explained, "Smoking. Smoked bacon?"

"I thought you were calling me a pig." Val shrugged as she turned back to look at her reflection. She had even put on makeup- well. Jess had done her makeup since Val was useless at eyeliner and needed to practise some more. She looked different than normal, but she didn't exactly hate it. She looked like a high school senior at least.

"I would never say that to you," Brock told her bluntly as he swung his legs around through Jess and so his feet were firmly on the ground. "You're stunning V. You just need to start owning it 'cause, as I told you two years ago, nothing is as sexy as confidence."

"Nothing is as freaky as talking to dead people." Val shot back, pursing her lips, and placing her hands on her hips. "And if we combine those two it's freaky sexy and that...doesn't sound sexy at all."

"These dead people," Jess gestured between her and Brock, "are your besties, your squad, and we are gonna totally hype you up all day. If you had just listened to me back when you were a freshman." Jess gave a dramatic sigh. "I could have had you knocked up by the quarterback right now!"

"Wooowowwww." Val and Brock both laughed.

"No teen pregnancies, thank you very much." Val moved to sit beside them both, sliding her feet into her 'prettier' combat boots with the roses embroidered on the side.

"No quarterbacks either. My Val has better taste than something that cliché." Brock wrinkled his nose as he swung his arm over Val's shoulder. Val rolled her eyes but didn't argue it as she tied her laces up.

"Brock...you were an athlete." Jess reminded him as she checked Val's phone for her when it buzzed. "Jenn's outside." Jess gently threw Val her phone as she sped through the double knot. Val headed for the door, the other two trailing behind her at a snail's pace. Val scooped up her backpack by the door and gave Oz a quick head scratch before padding down the front doorsteps and into Jenn's beat-up brown Volvo.

"Heyyyyyy." Jenn grinned as Val shut the door behind her. "So, I was gonna text you about it, but I thought you'd be more willing to give me the deets in person."

Jenn glanced over at Val as she pulled away from her spot. Val didn't have to ask her to elaborate. She knew exactly what she was talking about but now she wasn't exactly sure how to describe it.

James had left late last night. They watched the movie and talked and already had four inside jokes (James had counted) as well as a promise to meet up during their free period after lunch today to work on the project some more. The two had also been messaging from as soon as James had gotten home so Val hadn't collected as many clips for the project as she would have liked.

James had told her he could handle the editing stuff, really, but Val had insisted on at least finding the right clips and quotes for him. He had then distracted her with gifs of puppies, kittens and promises of fizzy candy that would feel like they were burning a hole in her tongue.

"Well, I don't think I'm gonna completely fail," Val said slowly "He's actually quite clever. He picked things up in the movie I'd never realised before."

Jenn let out a playful whistle. "You've watched that movie like a thousand times."

"I know. Surprised me too but I'd never noticed the stuff he was talking about. He was less Julia Stiles focussed and more background details." Val shrugged and shifted in her seat to get around a particularly uncomfortable spring that was underneath her.

While Jenn's car was drastically different from Val's sleek Jeep, Val loved riding passenger with her. Val had got her permit out of necessity rather than the love of driving and while her car had been an amazingly extravagant present from her parents, her best memories were with Jenn in this beat-up ugly brown disaster.

The two girls happily switched out who was driving the other to school on days where neither of them had late finishes or early starts. They weren't as frequent as they once were with all the extracurriculars that Jenn did to look good on a college application, but they were always more lively when they were singing along and messing around with a genuine CD player.

"Well, that makes sense. When he makes his social media content, he must have to check stuff like that. Can you imagine if he made videos in front of some cancelled artists' posters? It would just be so scandalous." Jenn dramatically placed a hand on her chest. "He may even lose his stalker fan club from it. My heart would *certainly* weep for him."

"All right give it a rest. We both know if we suddenly went viral, we would enjoy all the perks with it as well. I mean your Etsy would probably blow up along with you and then you haven't gotta tutor the nightmare child next door." Val gave a playful shudder. Jenn didn't have a comeback for that one.

Her tutoring side hustle usually wasn't too bad, but the best money-makers were the children whose parents never taught them basic manners. They tipped well and Jenn always said that was enough for her to keep going back. Her Etsy, full of her art prints and card designs, was sluggish at best, although Val always made a point of buying from her every holiday and when she had decorated her room last year.

"You got along with him, didn't you?" Jenn asked her softly. "I mean you're always really nice about people who don't deserve it but that was very defensive." Jenn once again glanced over at her as she stopped at a red light. Val felt her face flush slightly and she gave an awkward shrug.

"Well, then I'm sorry. I won't insult your new friend- unless he tries to take over the best friend role, in which case it's a competition and I take that very seriously. I need someone I can tag in super weird conspiracy theories without judgement." Jenn promised her as she started driving again.

"Um, she thinks she's your best friend?" Brock's head suddenly appeared in the space between the two girls' heads. "That's cute...maybe she should crash the car so we can have that conversation face to face. She's kinda cute if you like a big nose."

Val aggressively cleared her throat and turned to look at him, playing it off as looking out the back window. Brock got the message and mimed zipping and locking his mouth, throwing the invisible key over his shoulder.

If she had learned anything about Brock over the past three years, it was that he was jealous and generally spoke before he had thought anything through. He was right this time, however. Brock would be who Val considered her best friend; he was just not someone that Val could tell anyone about except her parents. In terms of alive, non-related humans, Jenn was definitely at the top of the list.

"Those conspiracy theories are freaky. I can't go into a gas station without checking to see if the dude behind the counter is a lizard person now!" Val laughed as Jenn pulled into a parking space on the school's lot. Jenn twisted her keys, and the car stopped its rumbling.

"Oh, if you're talking about the dude with the mullet, he is totally a lizard." Jenn nodded, unplugging her safety belt, and stepping out of her seat. Val followed gently shutting the passenger side door while Jenn slammed the driver's side.

"I'll see you at lunch." Jenn waved as she headed off to her homeroom.

"I'll buy the coffee." Val waved back as she headed in the opposite direction. Val had gone barely ten steps before she heard someone franticly running and slowing to a walk when they got next to her. She looked over, assuming she dropped something as she got out of the car, but all she saw was a beaming smile and a juice box being held out in front of her.

"I wasn't sure if you were an orange or apple person," James explained, "so I played it safe and went for summer berries."

James gave it a little shake as Val still hadn't taken it.

Val reached out and took the box with a growing smile and a "Well good morning to you too."

"I would have got coffee, but I didn't know what time you got here and that's a more complex question than a juice flavour." James came to a stop just outside the building door and Val stopped with him. He ran his hand through his hair and for the first time Val thought he looked awkward. The sight made her stomach flop to her feet. It looked so unnatural, like an unhappy child at Disneyworld.

"If this is you telling me you can't make the free period, you didn't have to get me this. It's fine: I'll just send you over what I've done tonight." Val told him softly and from the hurt look on James' face, she was wrong on his juice box intentions.

"That's not it," James told her quickly "actually I was wondering what your plans were for the lunch before the free period and if you maybe wouldn't completely object if I returned the food favour and bought you lunch."

"You don't have to do that. You got me a juice box. We're square." Val told him and poked the straw into the hole and took a long sip to prove her point. "I've just had like half of it, so no backsies now."

James looked like he was torn between sighing and laughing, and the result was a crooked little smile that was mostly in his eyes. "The juice box was just a nice gesture. Those are these things friends do for each other to show that they like each other and make each other feel good."

"You're very condescending considering we've only been friends...14 hours." Val mentally counted back the hours since he had sent her a friend request on Facebook. "You don't know what I do for my friends. I'm great around birthdays."

"Noted." James' smile turned into a smirk. "See, I'm great around Halloween and Christmas. All decorative holidays really."

"Noted," Val told him softly before taking another sip from her juice box.

Students started moving around them and James took a step forward so one could get past him holding a large bag, meaning he was toe to toe with Val. Val quickly took a step back making an awkward little noise as she did so.

As soon as that gap was created, Jess appeared into it and blocked James from view for the most part. "You GO on that date he just suggested, or I swear to god- "

"What, Jess?" Brock interrupted from behind Val, leaning his head forward to rest it on Val's shoulder as he stared at his former classmate. "You're gonna haunt her? Lil too late, dontcha think."

"You just think if she says no she's gonna magically decide she wants to date a dead guy and newsflash, Brock, you just feel like an ice block to her. James here is a nice and toasty hunk that can actually go out with her in public." Jess leant forward and sneered right in his face.

As the two ghosts started to bicker, Val realised that James was still just looking at her and the amused smile was back. Jess had moved slightly to continue her argument with Brock and the space she had left made it look as if Val had just spent the last thirty seconds staring at his chest. "I like your shirt," Val blurted out and instantly regretted it. It was a plain black long sleeve under a grey leather jacket. There was nothing special to like about it.

"Thanks." James responded, "I like your eyes."

"I got them from Target." Val quipped automatically, and James threw his head back and laughed.

Val had never thought about if she was funny or not, but hearing him laugh at a joke she made suddenly had her wishing she was a stand-up comedian. She could understand why all those people online just loved to watch him react to things.

After he had stopped messaging last night, she had given his socials a scroll, out of curiosity, and she had realised all over again how drop-dead gorgeous he was. The recorded laughs were nothing compared to hearing it in the first person. It was like watching grainy teenage Taylor Swift YouTube videos and then hearing her front row, a teasing echo of perfection.

"Walmart." James sighed dramatically as he tugged at the edge of his shirt. "I guess that makes us star-crossed lovers. Maybe we should have done Romeo and Juliet." James shot her a wink before ducking into the building and out of sight down the corridor.

Both the ghosts had gone silent although Val couldn't pinpoint when or who had won the argument. If it was about Brock's supposed feelings for her, she generally drowned it out. Brock flirted with everyone, even people that couldn't hear him, and Jess liked to push his buttons with anything she could.

"I can't believe you said no to that date," Jess whined as she peered around Val to try and catch a glimpse with him. "He's just so fine. I wanna cover him in chocolate and have him on pancakes."

"Cannibalism isn't very prom queen of you," Brock muttered.

Val sighed and headed inside taking a left rather than going straight down the corridor. She heard the two ghosts following her, bickering yet again but they were keeping it at a low volume at least. Jess didn't like to make Val snap or respond in public, and Val suspected it was because she felt bad for being the first ghost here to make her do it.

It had been Val's first day of freshman year and Jess had been beaming and squealing and grabbing all her ghost friends to show them the girl that could see them until eventually, Val had snapped at her to just shut the hell up in the middle of history. Mr Jenkinson had still never gotten over it and neither had the rest of the student body. That had been the birth of 'weirdo' and Jess's constant offers to make her pretty and popular. Now, in the January of her senior year, she was only just wearing a fully Jess-coordinated outfit.

As Val shuffled into her seat in homeroom, the two ghosts flocked to either side of her. There were times, especially after watching tv or listening to an intense playlist, that Val convinced herself that her ability was a good thing.

She could easily imagine them as a power trio with the right mindset and, as her mother had once awkwardly stated when trying to 'cheer her up,' if there was a CW show about a girl whose friends were ghosts, then she would lap it up. That thought was somewhat comforting; however, Brock had ruined it by calling her 'main character' and nothing else for a month afterwards.

"At least when he bails out, you'll have me and Jess to help you," Brock started brightly, in a way that made Val think they had been talking to her for the last few minutes and she'd just been too distracted to notice. Except Jess looked equally as confused about it.

Val scowled slightly as she pretended to look for something in her bag muttered, "He's not gonna bail out on me."

"Willing to bet on that? Movie night of winner's choice." Brock offered quickly.

"Deal." Val offered immediately, still in a mutter.

She wasn't sure why she was so confident that James would stay so focussed and involved, especially since he was being far too sweet in the beginning and that was never a good sign. But she believed it a hundred percent and if the worst thing to happen would be doing the project by herself and having to rewatch the scream movies with Brock, then it was a win-win situation for her anyway.

Chapter Four

Brock had been wrong about James' attention span. For the past four weeks, he had met her in the library for the free period and was sending her information after school as well. Two weeks in, the meet-up at free period turned into a meeting at lunch and staying together for the whole two hours.

The two would message back and forth constantly about everything they could think of. They knew each other's coffee orders and sandwich preferences, given each other multiple show and book recommendations, and now they were sat in front of a library computer, uploading their final file, and Val was wishing that the project had a deadline far further away than 3 pm.

The two had been silent ever since James had pressed the upload button. They had taken their time watching their video over and over, looking for anything to tweak or edit or cut to eat up the rest of the free period and put off what Val was expecting to be an awkward goodbye and then no contact ever again except maybe a small smile and good luck at graduation in a few months.

The progress bar suddenly shot forward from 32% to 54% and James leaned back in his chair. "So, it's Valentine's Day Friday." He looked over at Val.

Val just stared straight back at him, her brain suddenly lagging worse than the computer was as she tried to think of a response to that. It wasn't exactly a lot to go on conversation-wise.

"Yeah." Val decided on and then added, "Senior year seems to be just flying by, huh."

"Yeah.... actually, I was wondering if you had any plans on Friday. On Valentine's Day," James elaborated before he had even finished his initial sentence, as if Val hadn't quite understood that Friday was Valentine's Day.

"I usually watch some movies," Val said slowly. "The Coronet usually does a special event for it."

The Coronet was a dingey little cinema on the edge of town that was not quite arthouse but not mainstream. Their entire look was vintage, and it focused on staying that way. Val suspected it was because the owner thought it was cheaper to just keep deep cleaning and renovating the seats than to completely upgrade everything. It gave them a marketing niche to stay permanently in the nineties. Val saw that James was looking at her confused and realised that if he ever went to the movies, he probably went to the nice IMAX screens at the large chain cinema in the town centre.

"It's the little, outdated cinema on the way to Boston." Val elaborated and there seemed to be a flicker of recognition in James' eyes.

"Oh. I thought that got shut down ages ago." James looked more reserved than he had earlier, and he ran his hand through his hair. "I was, um, well, traditions do a special menu on Valentines Day that includes these cool milkshakes and I know you like over-the-top milkshakes so you should tell your date about it and maybe grab one before your movie because they look ridiculously unhealthy and – "

"I don't have a date," Val told him, and she felt her face and neck start to burn. "I usually go alone or with one of my parents if the other one is working, and they have Friday evening off together so it's just me." Val turned her attention towards the screen again. The progress bar was now moving slowly but consistently, currently at 72%.

She knew it was considered pathetic to spend Valentine's day alone, but she had always enjoyed it. Arguably she was never truly alone. Even now, Brock and Jess were milling around a nearby shelf and pretending not to be looking over and listening in.

Val risked a glanced over at James as he suddenly shifted in his seat and his knee bumped against her thigh. "So.... could I maybe join you? It's not the date I was gonna ask you on, but it sounds better actually."

Date. He was asking me out on a date. The thought echoed around Val's mind a few times as she turned her body to look at him, knees now clashing together but neither of them moved away.

"I didn't even tell you what movies are playing." Val smiled slightly.

She didn't have to look to see if Jess's interest had peaked. The air around Val had dipped a few degrees and the hairs on the back of her neck were standing up. The dead prom queen candidate had probably run straight through the tables and computers to get there in time to see Val's face.

"I'm not a picky movie person- well I am but I want to go on a date with you more than I don't want to watch *The Notebook* again," James told her softly.

His smile had disappeared for the most part and he was rubbing his hands together slowly in his lap, almost wringing them like a worried old maid in a fantasy tale.

"I don't like *The Notebook*. Not a fan of the ending." Val responded, her voice barely above a whisper. "It's, um, actually a horror theme night. *My Bloody Valentine* and *Ready or Not.* Those were the two I was gonna see...not very ideal first date on Valentine's Day material."

James perked up at that and his small smile turned into a face splitting grin as he argued, "No, I think it sounds perfect for us. I've never seen either of those. Did you wanna go for those milkshakes before? And the food of course. The actual dinner part of the dinner date I was asking you on. For the record in my head, the asking was a lot smoother and movie-magic like."

"I would love that." Val nodded at him and then let out a chuckle. "No, I think the asking was perfect for us. Anything smoother or more awkward and it wouldn't have worked out as well. Doesn't fit our dynamic duo vibe."

"Oh, I've been a bad influence on you." James leant forward, resting his elbows on his thighs, and supporting his head on his cupped hands. "You just used the word vibe. Next thing you know you'll be posting on your Instagram and maybe even lip-syncing to things on TikTok."

Val gasped and argued, "I post on my Instagram! Just.....not a lot."

She had posted on it only two weeks ago, a picture of Oz and her sat facing each other, both with treats on their noses. She thought it had been cute and it had received more likes than anything else in her profile. She wasn't a great hash tagger-it felt too awkward and unnatural- but she had been proud that her post's likes were in the triple figures and gained her a few new followers (all dog-based pages but still, those were the best kind of followers in her mind).

"Yeah, I saw the dog pic. Very cute. But do you always eat dog treats? Because it looks like you eat dog treats." James teased her, and Val rolled her eyes at him.

"Ya know, I can always take that date back." Val threatened, although it was clear to both of them that it was an empty one. The last time Val had been on a date it was back in Chicago and the phrase 'date' meant a lot different to an eighteen-year-old than it did to a fourteen-year-old.

They had only just started talking about it but already there was a bubble of excitement and nerves in Val's stomach. She was going on a date, in her senior year, and it was with a ridiculously gorgeous nerd with cheekbones to rival Angelina Jolie's. Maybe she was the main character after all.

Chapter Five

The rest of the week passed in the blink of an eye. Jess was organising her outfits and her makeup every day. Val felt like a real-life barbie doll, but she wasn't about to complain. Brock sulked for a little while, complaining about the fact that their Valentine's Day plans were now ruined.

He had stopped whining relatively quickly and gone back to his usual self, if a little softer. The compliments in the morning were less crude. Val was gorgeous rather than sexy, she looked pretty rather than smoking. Whatever Jess had said to him, and Val was sure that she must have said something, it had clearly struck a chord.

Jess had picked out an outfit that was perfect for school and a date, but Val was almost certain that she had never seen it before in her life, let alone bought it for herself. It was a red minidress, long-sleeved with a swooping neckline, and it was tight. Val didn't mind that though which surprised her, and she even took a few photos in it that she would debate about posting later.

She opened up her bedroom door, chatting away to Brock and Jess about rules for the date tonight. They could sit nearby, of course, and whenever she could Val would respond but she wasn't going to outright talk back to them like she usually did when they were at The Coronet.

The busiest Val had ever seen the cinema was at maybe 25% capacity and it only had three screens with a scattering of viewing times on any day that wasn't a holiday. It made it perfect for talking to her unseen friends and making them all feel a little more normal.

The two ghosts told her that the Coronet was incredibly popular back when they were alive and that they had both lined up for a whole day to get in and get tickets for Scream when it was released. The two had rarely spent time together when they were alive, more casual acquaintances than friends, so Val had assumed that it had been quite an event if they had both been there.

Val came to a stop just in the doorway and let out a breezy chuckle. A few inches from her feet was a large box of chocolate with a ribbon on the front. On top was a rainbow rose, its petals a swirl of different colours and a cream envelope with her name scrawled across it in gorgeous calligraphy.

Val crouched down picking up the gifts as she headed downstairs. They were a Valentine's tradition from her father. The rose was rainbow ever since Val's obsession with unicorns at the age of four, but the large chocolate selection had always been the same. Val was specific about the type of chocolate that she liked, and it was very rare to find a selection box she could fully eat. They had found only one, from a little chocolate shop in Chicago, and its cute little logo of a crown in the top right corner told Val that this box was from the same shop.

Once they were downstairs and in the living room, Val saw that there were two little gift bags on the table. Her mother would have been given her Valentine presents up in the bedroom, usually things that were elaborate, expensive, and sentimental at the same time. Her father was always very good at buying presents and her mother was good at experiences. She usually gifted her husband with trips or days out rather than material things. It was a dynamic that worked between them, and Val had always found it incredibly sweet how their approaches were completely different but never failed.

"Oh, he shouldn't have," Jess said softly as she slowly reached out to finger the bow on the gift bag marked with her name. Brock was silent as he walked over to his own and gently pulled it open. Brock's bag had a special collector's edition figurine from his favourite childhood tv show and the teenage boy's eyes looked a little misty as he looked down at it.

Brock had been popular in school but according to Jess, before she had talked to him as a ghost, she had never known he was actually into anything besides drinking and whatever boys did when they hung out together. Val gave them a moment to look through their bags and found her father silently reading the news on his phone as he sipped his coffee at the kitchen table.

Daniel Ellis was an attractive surgeon, tousled hair the colour of charcoal with a constant matching stubble and emerald, green eyes that always seemed too bright to be natural. Val's friends back in Chicago had always told her that their mothers thought he was a 'dilf' and it had taken her far too long to realise that they wore low cut tops or short skirts whenever they popped by.

Val had spent that night in front of a mirror, prodding at her face and trying to see more of her father in her features. She had inherited his hair, but her eyes were a slightly darker, moss green and her face was rounder, more like her mother's.

Her mother wasn't ugly, but the world critiqued women more than it did men, and when your husband was Daniel

Ellis, they expected even more. They expected his wife to be super skinny and blonde and chiselled and while Charlotte Ellis was blonde, that was the only part that matched. Her face was round, her nose slightly crooked, and while her weight fluctuated a bit depending on her shift patterns, she had never been under a size fourteen, even before giving birth.

"You look lovely," Daniel told his daughter as he glanced up from his article. Val picked up the coffee pot on the side and poured the remains into the nearest mug. She reached over for some milk and added plenty of sugar.

"Thanks." Val smiled as she sat next to him. "Thank you for the gifts. I haven't opened the card yet, but I'm excited about the drawing." The Valentines Day card was always signed the same, but the animal badly drawn next to it changed every year.

Val took a sip of her coffee and then gave it another stir. "I thought Brock was going to cry when he saw that figurine. Did you have a little eBay shopping spree again?"

"Something like that," Daniel agreed with a laugh. "Did Jess like hers?"

"She hadn't opened hers when I came in. I thought I'd give them a little space and grab some breakfast."

"Val, you've only made a coffee." Daniel pointed out and raised both his eyebrows at her.

"That's breakfast!" Val insisted and looked him in the eye as she took a long gulp from her mug. Daniel rolled his eyes and then stood up from his seat and started to make her some toast.

"So what time is James picking you up?" he asked as he slid the bread into the holes. He had taken the news that Val had a date surprisingly well considering her mother was now on shift most of the day and they would have to have a late dinner together. "I know it's not exactly romantic, but you could always drive separately for the day."

"We are going straight to dinner after school. It makes no sense for us to both waste gas and both pay parking." Val reminded her father.

Val had thought it was quite sweet that James offered to drive her to school and around all day. Jess had thought so as well, and Brock had sweetly reminded them that if James did anything creepy in the car Brock would make it crash. The threat had been quite comforting.

"Sure sure." Her father agreed with a small head nod as he turned to grab the hot, freshly toasted bread as it popped up. He was lightning quick to grab a stick of butter from the fridge, cutting off a small square to spread across. "Just call me old-fashioned but- "

"I don't think it's old-fashioned for you to want your daughter to drive herself everywhere. I think it's actually the opposite." Val interrupted. Her father shot her a look and Val grinned back.

"Okay fine. I just...I know it's hard, but it is going to get better I promise." Val's father began, and Val was tempted to interrupt him again to finish off the speech she had heard a hundred times.

Every time she came back from school a little glum, every time they had gone out as a family and someone around her age had looked at her a little weirdly, Val's father came to her with food or a hot drink and a 'comforting' reminder that people were a lot crueller when she was younger and when she became an adult, no one was going to care if she looked into mid-air.

Val took the plate he was offering, and half zoned out as she took a large bite. She listened just enough to nod at the right time and make an agreeable noise. He mentioned college. She took a larger thoughtful bite. She had been looking at Harvard ever since he had given her the speech the first time, after a field trip to the zoo when she was twelve and she had screamed when she caught sight of a drowned child in the penguin enclosure. Val suspected that's why her parents snapped this place up rather than somewhere sunnier by a beach.

The proximity to the ivy league had swayed them and probably was what her mother was focusing on when looking up the local tragedies. That and the dreadful online news coverage of the shooting meant Val had walked into the school completely blindsided.

Practically nothing about it had been uploaded or written about online and Val's research about it came from the school and local libraries. She had stolen most of it three years ago. The town had forgotten the teenage victims until it came to facing their remaining parents in supermarkets or town events. Then it was a hushed 'So sad what happened' between themselves after unsubtle glances and a brief, inaccurate 'Their child passed away.'

Their children hadn't passed away. They hadn't died. They had been ripped away; they had been murdered. They were all but forgotten to the outside world.

"I'm going to go to the DIY store tomorrow," Val decided out loud after finishing off her toast and her father's soft 'it gets better kid' smile turned sad. "Ya know, if you have anything I can pretend to need."

"Well, we could always use more nails," Val's father joked dryly before sipping his coffee. "Tell him I'm building myself a new desk. That should keep you busy for a few visits at least. I take it you've already booked a new hair appointment then?"

"I'm going Wednesday after school. The last time I was there she reminded me how quickly her prom slots go so I'll book in for that as well." Val started examining her finger-nails, freshly varnished in black with little red heart stickers that Jess had magically found and applied for her last night.

"Prom isn't until June, right?"

"Teenage girls are crazy. Some of them are already trying to campaign for prom queen and applications aren't in until May! I don't get it. If you want a glittery plastic crown and a half-dead bouquet that badly, go to Walmart."

"But you still plan on going?" Daniel Ellis's voice was tinged with amusement and Val shot a pout in his direction.

"Jess and Brock wouldn't let me skip it even if I died," Val stated and while her father didn't look particularly im-pressed with the comment, he was saved from commenting by the two undead teenagers' entrance into the kitchen.

"Oh, Danny, you spoilt us this year." Jess gushed as she ran over and threw her arms around Val's father's neck. "I love it! And Brock loves his too, even though he'd never admit it."

"It was awesome, Mr E. Thanks a lot." Brock piped up as he swivelled a kitchen chair around and sat on it, arms crossed over the back. If it weren't for the gory wound and blood-stained shirt, he would look straight out of a made-for-school video about how not to act in a classroom.

"You kids are welcome." Daniel smiled at them both. It had never felt weird to them that Daniel called them kids, although if they had survived they would have been of similar ages. At least, they had never mentioned it to Val. She assumed it was because of her father's expert social skills.

She had seen him at work, and he could flip between situations so confidently and so completely you would never have known he lost a patient that morning with how he cooed over a child's superman shirt that very afternoon.

"Has Val told you all about tonight? You and Charlie are gonna have the house all to yourselves!" Jess chattered as she moved to sit in the chair beside the doctor. "Well, until midnight when we will make sure that Val will come straight home because that's her curfew." Jess made a gesture as if she were crossing her heart. "But that's plenty of time for a romantic dinner with your gorgeous wife. What did you get her for Valentine's Day?"

As Jess and Daniel split off into their conversation, Brock locked eyes with Val and then gave them a playful roll. Val grinned back at him before finishing the rest of her coffee in one gulp.

A glance at her phone told her James would be here in the next few minutes and while he had met her dad during one of their study sessions at her house, she wasn't going to risk it before a date.

The situation seemed different, there was more tension around it even though the actual introduction was out of the way. Val placed her dirty plate and mug in the sink, kissing her father's cheek as she walked past without breaking his conversation with Jess.

Jess would follow or appear at school whenever she wanted and from the looks of it, that would be whenever Daniel had to go and do something else. Val didn't expect

Brock to stay with her after his previous attitude towards today, but he got up and followed her to the front door, grabbing her bag and jacket for her before she could.

"I heard you say about the shop. Thanks." Brock told her softly as he walked directly behind her and slipped the items into her hand. "Holidays are rough for me, even stupid ones like Valentine's Day."

Val didn't have to turn around to guess that Brock was rubbing his hand over the back of his head and looking away from her. It was an awkward subject for him, and Val tried to make it as natural as possible.

"Of course," Val whispered to him as she opened up the front door and immediately shivered. The air was a lot brisker than she had thought. She took a big step forward and then started digging around for her keys in the side pocket of her bag. "I like going anyway. I don't know what half the stuff is even for, but that's where you come in," Val teased him.

She didn't know anything about screwdrivers, but she knew that she had every type you could physically have and whenever something did get broken in the house (a frequent occurrence, considering half the house's inhabitants made things fly through the air when they are upset), Brock was there to fix it anyway.

Val's mother had playfully called him Claire's handyman after the dead cheerleader had a particularly bad tantrum on the last anniversary of her death and destroyed the entire bookcase. She had quickly been gestured by Val to stop, but the damage had been done. Claire had spent a week breaking things just to watch Brock fix them for the Ellis family. It had only been when Jess expressed her displeasure to Claire about it that she stopped.

"Loverboy is here," Brock told her bitterly and Val looked towards the road. She hadn't heard any cars pull up. "He has been for.... I don't know, like, five minutes. I heard him pull up."

"Ghosts have super hearing now?" Val quipped under her breath as she shot her date a wave and headed down the steps towards his car. Brock let out a sarcastic 'ha ha' before padding down the stairs with her.

"I can literally teleport anywhere I like because I have no physical body and it's my hearing you get all weirded out by. You're so strange, Val," Brock said lovingly.

Val shot him a soft smile under the guise of looking back at her house to make sure the door was shut. When she looked back to the car, James had gotten out of his side and was now leaning against the passenger door. As she got close enough, he opened up the door for her in dramatic fashion.

"How very gentlemanly of you." Val adjusted the bag strap on her shoulder.

James didn't respond, just grinned, and opened the door slightly wider. As Val got closer, she realised there was something in the passenger seat. It was a bright red something against gorgeous black leather seats. The whole car was gorgeous. It was gleaming in the weak sunlight, making its way through the dense grey clouds in the sky and its body was painted a dark blue that reminded Val of spilt biro ink. Val didn't know the exact model, but she recognised the Honda symbol on the front. It looked like James had it recently cleaned. Val was oddly touched he went to such an effort.

Val burst into laughter as she become level with James and saw clearly what was on her seat. There were two gifts and a card and Val shot him an amused look as she reached forward to pick them up.

It was a medium-size plush of a ladybug holding a large heart in its hands that had *Happy Valentine's Day* embroidered in gold. There was a rose lodged in-between the arm and heart except when Val looked at it wasn't a normal rose. The red was just foil and there were no actual petals.

"I was stuck between chocolate and roses, so I figured...chocolate rose." James beamed at her, and Val hugged the ladybug. She heard Brock mutter something behind her, but she didn't quite catch what.

"That's very sweet of you but you didn't have to," Val told him as she climbed into the car.

"It's Valentine's day. It's our first date. You already bought the tickets for tonight before I even had a chance, so this is the least I could do," James argued as he shut her door for her and then walked around to his sit to hop into the driver's seat.

Once he was in and the engine was on, Val watched him for a second. He looked like he was glowing from the inside out and Val had never seen him without at least a small smile on his face. If she ever saw him genuinely frown, she was sure it would be the sign of the apocalypse.

"Do I have something on my face?" James interrupted her ogling and she quickly focussed out of the window in front of her. She felt her face heat up slightly as she shook her head. "I don't think I'm a messy eater either but the place I told you about has some awesome ribs so.... I know it's bad to date etiquette to have ribs but I'm just throwing it out there that I may check as a genuine question later on. Also, if you get something more than a salad then that's fine too and I don't want you doing that thing girls do where they undereat."

"Oh, there's no worry about that." Brock snorted from his place in the backseat, even leaning forward to pop his head in between the other two. "Remember the last thanksgiving? You had like half the turkey."

Val clenched her jaw quickly and then shot James a smile. "I don't see the point in ordering a salad at a restaurant. Unless it's, ya know, a loaded salad with chicken or prawns or something."

"This is the beginning of your first date and you're talking salads," Brock said bluntly "When I would take a girl on a first date, there was no talk about salads. This dude is as manly as one-ply paper, Val, come on."

Val wanted to roll her eyes and snap at him- it made him less manly because he brought up a salad? - but instead, she took a deep breath and looked down at her gift. "I just got it- it's a love bug. Clever." Val chuckled, and James laughed with her.

"I thought that and the rose was quite witty," James admitted as they came to a red light. "I figured witty was your type." James looked over at her and at Val's confused look he added awkwardly "You laugh a little whenever we have to read Shakespeare and he's all about wordplay. It's kinda under your breath or sometimes you just kinda smirk at a certain bit... I'm not helping myself not look like a creep, am I?"

"Incredibly creepy," Brock grumbled at the same time as Val replied, "That one was sweet." James shot her a disbelieving look and Val insisted, "That you noticed and acted on it. I didn't realise I did that and you're right: I'm a sucker for wit."

James opened his mouth as if he was going to say something else but then the car behind them gave a loud honk and James swore under his breath and quickly started driving again as he realised the light had turned green. Val's lips twitched into a smile, but she pressed her lips together to stop it.

"I usually notice when the lights... change." James defended lamely.

"Oh my god Val please do not get in this car again. We can walk home. Me and you can get dinner and watch a movie. Do not date this clown," Brock begged from the backseat, now hunched over and scowling.

"It's okay. I can't do roundabouts. Well, I can but I hate them, so I pick the route with less of them," Val babbled back to make him feel better.

It wasn't exactly a lie: she did hate roundabouts, but she also never really went anywhere where there would be masses of them. If she was heading into Boston, then she was usually with one of her parents or with Jennifer.

"That makes me feel better. Thank you." James said softly as he indicated left into the high schools parking lot.

Val started to awkwardly put the gifts into her bag, trying not to just shove them into the available space. Eventually, she rejigged her books to make some space at the front and she would just carry the rose until she could eat it or put it in her locker.

James parked up and then turned to look at her with one hand still on the wheel. "So, I have some stuff I've gotta do at lunch today. If I don't see you, I'll text you."

"We have English together." Val reminded him as she slowly undid her seatbelt. "It's how we met. You may remember it as the class that watches movies a lot."

James rolled his eyes at her and shook his head smiling. "I don't see class as prime couple time. You may remember there's this thing called a teacher there and they talk a lot."

Val and James locked eyes. Val was tempted to latch onto that word- *couple*. But it was clear he was looking for a reaction and Val didn't want to look as if she was already head over heels for him, even though the word sent her stomach into a horde of butterflies.

"Yeah, I remember. I'm the one with perfect attendance and you're the one who skips to film dance videos in the hall." Val leant towards him as she responded softly.

"Oh, you've seen the dance videos, huh?" James leant forward as well matching the distance she had moved and not a centimetre more. "What did you think of my sick moves?"

"I saw the one where you slipped and fell on your face."

"Well, that's the viral one so...makes sense," James responded instantly, not phased at her response.

Val smirked at him, and her eyes caught on his lips for a just second, but then he was grinning at her with his paper white teeth.

"Get out the car, Val," Brock piped up. "You don't wanna be late and I don't wanna see this. I can't puke but I can try."

Val pulled back and picked up her bag again. "I should get to class. Thanks for the lift." Val reached out to open the door, shooting him a smile over her shoulder as she did so while Brock kept shooing her out. It was only when she was a few feet away and heading into the main building that she slid her earphones in, holding up the mic section so she would look like she was on a phone call.

"You didn't have to be such a dick about it. It's Valentine's Day." Val looked up and around the entrance. Pink and red streamers had been hung over the entrance, origami hearts pinned onto the walls and hanging from the ceiling. They had also dusted off a small, badly painted cupid statue and placed it on the reception desk next to a vase full of fabric roses that weren't fooling anybody.

"I think that thing was here when I was still actually attending class. I'm pretty sure some kid in art class made it. You reckon if I pick it up there's gonna be initials on its feet?" Brock called to her as he ignored her comment and walked over to the desk and examined the statue up close. Val kept walking in the direction of her locker.

"Do not pick that up?" Val said, and she shimmied her shoulders to adjust her bag straps without dropping the earphone. It still amazed her that all she had to do was hold a part of an earphone up to her mouth and speak for people to not even look at her. If she was speaking softly, under her breath without the prop, then people looked at her as if she was insane.

She sometimes wondered if her father's school days had been as dreadful as he pretended they were since he didn't have such technology back then. He was forever joking about how he didn't even have a brick phone until he was already a resident and how that would have been his saviour. But then she saw him charming anyone he meets, and she realised even in high school he would be smooth and at the worst below everyone's radar.

"You're boring now," Brock whined as he hurried to catch up with her. He even slung his arm over Val's shoulder and Val breathed out a laugh.

"I've always been boring," Val said in a sing-song voice. "I would love to be boring and below the radar and... beige."

"Below the radar is overrated. You are special with a gift and that gift has brought you a friendship with me and that right there is priceless," Brock responded without even a heartbeat thought.

"Ya know I don't think it's a gift when it's the whole reason I'm traumatised for life."

"You think my wound is sexy don't try and pull that."

"Hmmm blood and gore, that's my kink right there," Val said dryly, and she saw someone shoot her a bizarre look from the corner of her eye. Val smiled at them, but they had already turned back to their locker. Brock shot her an overly dramatic pout.

"I still say we should make out just to see if we can. Ya know, for science." Brock shimmied his shoulders as he removed his arm from her shoulders when they got to her locker.

Jenn's locker was next door, and the petite goth girl was cheerfully reading something behind the door. Jess was leaning against the door of the locker on Jenn's other side, creating a kind of sandwich of the three girls with Jenn in the middle.

"She's got a Valentine's card!" Jess gushed when she caught sight of Brock and Val and from the look on her face, it was as if Jess herself had received one. Jess had always had a particular soft spot for Jennifer, even going so far as to take revenge on a far too bold boy who had referred to Jennifer as the N-word back in freshman year. That had been the catalyst for Val and Jess's friendship. Jennifer had assumed it was Val who had shut the cupboard door on his hand, so he had to go to the nurse.

"Oh, hey Val!" Jenn beamed over at her, sliding the card back into the envelope and shutting her locker door. "Happy V Day!"

"Happy V Day!" Val chirped back as she unlocked her locker, having to give it a little whack to get it unstuck. "Who's the card- oh." Val stopped mid-sentence as a bright pink envelope fluttered out of her locker. Val crouched down to pick it up.

"Oh, you got one too! They must have been in school so early to deliver all of them to everyone's lockers. Linda Earl said they sold over two hundred this year, so prom's already got a decent budget." Jenn beamed.

Jenn's genuine happiness for others clashed with her dark eye makeup and ripped mesh top, and when Val was back up standing and opening her Valentine's Day card, Jenn was watching her as if she was about to unlock the secret of immortality.

"So." Val carefully opened up the seal on her card, her face already turning slightly red. James wouldn't have given her another card, would he? Not when he had given her one with the presents earlier. "Who was yours from?" She should have at least got him a card. She should have thought to fill out one of those sales forms for these cards and got one dropped off at his locker.

"Just says a secret admirer. I think I recognise the hand-writing though." Jenn's voice turned coy for a moment before she continued cheerfully, "What about yours? James seems like the type to send something."

Val nodded in agreement, expecting to see James' intricate scrawl and a funny anecdote but instead there were incredibly neat letters and a heartfelt line.

Happy Valentine's Day Gorgeous.

Val immediately turned her head to look at him, her face softening. Brock was shooting her a sad smile. She couldn't outright ask him why, but he simply shrugged at her in answer to the question anyway.

Val turned her head back to Jess and Jenn, both watching her with intrigued expressions. "Not James," Val told them as she carefully slid the card back into her locker and then started to swap out her books.

Jenn let out an amused little laugh as she saw the lovebug toy and the two started chattering about their plans for the night, projects, and the weekend as they headed to class.

Val tried to talk to Jenn about the card she had gotten but she didn't want to say whom she thought it was from and Val could respect that. Jenn was smiling and as long as she was happy then so was Val. Jenn did ask who Val's locker card was from, even suggesting it was from Dylan.

Dylan was a mutual friend who throws get-togethers whenever his father is out of town which was at least once a month. He was Jenn's friend since middle school, and they had bonded over passionate Panic! At the Disco discussions. Jenn had spent the last few years subtly and not so subtly hinting to Val that he was into her but always respected when Val showed no interest.

Val was just telling her that 'No, it wasn't Dylan' when they got to their homeroom and the conversation was cut short. Dylan was in the corner, overhead earphones blasting out something with heavy bass. The two girls shot him a smile as they sat down, and Jenn shot Val a playful wink.

Chapter Six

"He's now ten minutes late. Let's just go without him." Brock piped up from his spot on the hood of James' car. He had made the same complaint every minute that James had been late, and Jess was rolling her eyes at him every time.

"When we get to the restaurant, we will leave you and James alone," Jess promised as she jumped up next to Brock and swung her legs back and forth. "It's not gonna be much of a first date if you have us crowding your space."

"But we will be sitting next to you for the movies. It's not a movie night without my witty commentary." Brock leant back on his elbows, head resting back against the windshield as if it were his bed and not the front of a car. Val thought that it couldn't have been comfortable, but he looked completely at ease.

"Witty is not the word I would use to describe your commentary. Crude, repetitive maybe." Val smirked over at him, and Brock tilted his head so she could see him raise an eyebrow at her. Val raised one back. The car park was full of students milling around and her earbuds were firmly jammed into her ears, so no one was looking particularly hard at her. The two stayed like that, each one refusing to look away.

"Here he comes! Oh, and he has a gift bag." Jess hopped off of the car and moved to stand by Val as if James would be able to see her as well. "Betcha five bucks that's why he's late."

"Jess, you don't have any money." Val reminded her softly as she watched James catch sight of her, wave, and start to jog over to her.

"I'm so sorry you've been waiting," James told her quickly as he skidded to a stop in front of her. The other students just seemed to move out of his way automatically, turning to look at what he was in such a rush to get to. The answer seemed to disappoint more than a few of them, their faces shifting into confusion and then within seconds they were completely disinterested and turning back to their own lives.

"I was heading out of class and then," James looked down at the bag in his hand, "this thing happened, and it wasn't something I could just leave and.....that's totally something you're gonna want me to explain because that seems super sketchy now I've said it like that. I'll explain in the car if you like." James finished up his little ramble with a smile and his hand started rooting around in his pockets for the car keys.

"It sounds like a hell of a story." Val chuckled as she opened up the passenger side door and climbed in.

James let out an exasperated sigh of agreement as he climbed into the seat next to her. He turned and placed the gift bag in the backseat, right through Brock's lap. Brock gaped at him for a second and then it turned into a scowl as he slid himself into the middle seat instead.

"It's going to come off incredibly cocky," James warned her as he started the car up and pulled out of his spot. "But the reason it took me a while to get out of class is that this girl was waiting outside my final class with that stuff, and I had to tell her I was flattered but couldn't take it because

I'm seeing someone and well she kinda cried and I couldn't just leave her there crying in the hallway."

"Seeing someone, huh?" Val blurted out and James shot her a look that was somewhere between panic and amusement.

"Are we...not?" James questioned softly. "You didn't argue this morning when I said the couple, so I just assumed, I guess. Sorry."

"No-no, I didn't mean it like that."

"So, we are seeing each other."

"We see each other quite a lot."

"You're hilarious. Should I have put in that card an official question? Just to save us this *what are we* conversation while I have another girl's presents and secret admirer cards in the backseat?" James' words were mocking but his tone didn't match.

It sounded like he was nervous and covering it up with a decent game face. His eyes were remaining solely on the road and Val already knew his driving well enough to know that wasn't his usual style. He hadn't even turned his music on when he got in and he wasn't reaching over to do so as they left the campus.

"I didn't even get you a card." Val pointed out softly, speaking slowly as she tried to savour the moment. "So, it's not exactly a notch in the good girlfriend column. Maybe I'll do better next year, or we can send an email. Save the trees."

James' face lit up into a large grin that took up most of his face and he reached over to take her hand in his. "I accepted a gift from another girl. I would offer them to you instead, but I don't think you want a *world's cutest influencer* mug."

Val threw her head back and laughed. "Well, you are pretty cute."

The rest of the drive was full of laughter, blasting top forty hits and multiple glances that ended up catching the other looking. Brock and Jess stayed in the back, singing along, and dancing no matter what came on.

Val knew that James couldn't see her friends and couldn't hear Brock dramatically screaming along to the breakup lyrics and she tried not to keep looking back at them, but they were happy and that thought made Val smile even wider.

Jess and Brock stayed true to their word and stayed away from the couple when they got to the restaurant. They headed to sit on the stalls in front of the counter while James and Val slid themselves into a booth. The restaurant was themed like a 50s diner and Val half expected for the waitress to be wearing roller skates to match her baby blue dress with the white frilly apron.

For Valentine's Day, the diner had laid out menus in the shape of a heart, salt and pepper shakers shaped like cupids, and the windows had vinyl plastered on them with various lyrics or quotes about love.

James and Val were sat by the window, underneath a large vinyl reminding them that 'you walked in, and my heart went boom!' It was cute and couples around them were snapping videos and photos as equally cute food was brought out to them- including the milkshakes James had mentioned.

"Oh my god, they are massive!" Val laughed as she caught sight of a glass the size of her head being brought out to a table nearby. It was covered with sprinkles and whipped cream and there was a large lollipop stuck into the side as well. James grinned at her as he played with the edges of the laminated menu.

"The normal ones are great as well. They have special ones for all kinds of holidays. Fourth of July is layered all the different colours and has a little flag in it." James mused. Val leaned back in her chair and looked down at the menu.

"The soulmate shake." Val read out loud. "Candyfloss flavoured milkshake topped with whipped cream, heart-shaped strawberry sprinkles, and garnished with two edible straws."

"How ocean-friendly." James purred as he flipped the menu over to look at the back. "Don't worry, I'm not gonna steal any of your shakes. I'm thinking I grab one of those infused sodas they have here. That and this heartbreak hamburger." James looked up at her above the menu and Val glanced down at her own.

"The 'what a catch carbonara' looks nice." Val put her menu down and James nodded at her before reaching over to scan a QR code on the end of the table and order the meals. Val thought that was a much better system than keeping extra staff behind the counter, stuck behind the register.

The girl behind the counter looked stressed enough already getting all the drinks prepared and cakes from the display case presented nicely. Brock was watching her with intense interest while Jess was trying to subtly help without appearing like things were moving by themselves.

"So," James said as he put his phone down, "what kinda popcorn girl are you? Sweet? Salted? Mixed?" James' fingers started to play with the edges of the laminate menu, bending it back and forth as he looked at her.

Don't play with your fingers. It means you're nervous and nervous isn't hot, Jess's voice echoed inside Val's brain. She had told her that years ago when trying to be helpful. Val hadn't listened to her then and she was surprised that she had even remembered it. Was James nervous? He did look out of place. It was like watching a Greek God shuffle his feet around a train station, such a bland background for someone so radiant.

The girls at school called him a star because of how popular he was online, and Val could agree with the description but not for the same reason. James was a star because he was a beacon of light, more subtle than a sunbeam but much more constant.

"Mixed." Val responded, "but I'm not fussy."

"I like mixed as well. People think that's weird, ya know." James' eyes caught hers and there was his signature twinkle. He stopped playing with the edge of the laminate and his hand lay flat against the table, halfway across. Val leant forward and her fingertips brushed against his.

"People think I'm weird too." Val joked. "Maybe you're just into weird things."

James opened his mouth to answer, but the waitress has arrived with the drinks and they both thanked her as they were placed on the table. Val slowly spun her glass and admired the milkshake. She looked up from it and back to James to make a joke that the milkshake itself was her soulmate and found herself looking at his phone.

"I won't post it," James told her softly as he lowered it again. "I just...you looked really cute." He put the phone next to his drink shamefully. Val tilted her head slightly and then gave a side-eye glance at her milkshake.

"Can I see it? I wanna see how crazy I look." Val joked, and James reopened his phone and slid it across to her to see. It wasn't a photo like Val thought it would be, but a short video of her looking at the glass and smiling softly. "You can post it.... or send it to me and I'll post it." Val slid his phone back across to him and James was smiling at her.

"I'll make an influencer out of you yet," James told her as he quickly forwarded the video to her and then, with a glance up through his lashes at her, opened up his Instagram as well.

The rest of the dinner was also full of photos and videos. Val took some of James in both serious and funny poses, they even took pictures and videos of the food and then Val took videos of James dancing as he drove them to the cinema afterwards. At the cinema, the two split up, Val heading towards the ticket counter to collect the tickets she had preordered while James headed towards the snack counter.

The cinema had a high ceiling that was intricately etched with drawings. They looked straight out of a movie, like the stone carvings so often shown during fantasies to introduce a villain's backstory. The walls were all painted a light stone grey, and the floor was a bright red carpet as if every showing was a premiere. While the theme for the place was retro, the screens were still good everything was clean and up to standard. It had personality, which Val felt the large chains didn't.

"Hey, Sarah." Val greeted brightly after her short wait behind a middle-aged couple who had collected their tickets and then moved to the side. The cashier was dressed up in a gorgeous red dress with a sweetheart neckline, blonde hair pulled back into a messy bun with tendrils framing her face. The only thing that showed her as working was the black lanyard around her neck and a clapperboard shaped name tag.

"Hey, Val," Sarah responded as she slid the cash drawer shut and she started to thumb through the envelopes in a container to the side. "There you are. Two tickets this time. Your dad parking the car or something?"

"I gotta date actually," Val told her with a grin as Sarah handed over the tickets. "He's just grabbing the snacks." As soon as Val said that, Sarah was leaning over the counter and craning her head to get a look at the snacks section.

"He's hot!" Sarah declared as she caught sight of the only man there without a partner. James was making conversation with Theo, a boy in the year below them that suffered from terrible acne, as he placed the snacks on the counter. Val looked at Sarah, whose face matched her shocked tone and Val awkwardly agreed before making her way over to James without a goodbye.

"Val! Hey!" Theo greeted her warmly as she came to a stop next to James. "I thought I saw your name on the system." Val shot the boy a smile and her face felt particularly warm as James slung his arm over her shoulders. It made it particularly difficult for him to grab the popcorn and the drinks, but Val was quick to grab the drinks for him with an awkward smile at Theo and a quick goodbye.

Val half expected Brock or Jess to make a teasing comment in her ear about Theo and she subtly glanced around but found the two of them staring intently at the couple to the side. Brock was staring intensely at the poor man's face. Brock and Jess were muttering to each other, getting louder and more heated as Val approached.

"I'm telling you that's him." Jess hissed, arms crossed and her face set in a rare scowl.

"It's not." Brock snapped as he pulled back from the couple and waved a hand in false disinterest. "He's too old."

"He's not," Jess whispered. "Brock, he's not." Jess's scowl cracked, and her face twisted into something Val had never seen before, on living or the dead. It was heartbreak, anger, and grief all mixed up with a sad smile of acceptance.

It took Val a moment: they were already getting their tickets checked and heading to their screen before she realised why that look was on Jess's face and what it meant, what they had been discussing. Val's heart broke for them. It was one of the multiple moments over multiple years when the teenager's tragedy would slice at her.

The first time Val had ever seen their memorial pages in the yearbook. Brock's absolute fascination when a new gaming console came out. Jess's horror when she realised the song on the radio that she remembered from her childhood was during a 'throwback' set. Now, this- the two seeing a friend of theirs from their youths all grown up. Something they would never be.

Chapter Seven

"Brock, do you think this is the best...." Val trailed off as she turned her head to look at her best friend in the passenger seat. They were parked up outside his family's DIY store, as she had promised, but Brock had been in a sombre mood ever since the movies. He had given only half-hearted commentary and his eyes had been on the adult couple more than they had the screen. Every little kiss and nuzzle between them had Brock flinching as if he was being attacked.

Brock's face was a mirror of Jess's, but it lacked the smile. His jaw was clenched, and he was angrier than she had been, at least on the outside. Val had been on the edge of her seat the entire night, waiting for Brock to snap and scream or cry, but he never had. She felt like a bomb dog, sniffing around trying to find the detonator.

"Okay," Val breathed and opened up the car door, hesitating for a second to see if Brock would argue or say something to her. There was nothing and when Val turned her head and faced the front of the store, Brock was already leaning against that doorframe and watching her. "You know that freaks me out," Val muttered as she locked her car and walked past him.

The store had a small bell at the top that let out a pleasant little ding as Val and Brock stepped inside. The store was warm, in temperature and décor. The walls were painted a light yellow with dark mahogany flooring. The shelves holding the store's inventory were all handmade, attached to the walls or as structures that created aisles big enough for three people to walk through. The shop was in the shape of a perfect square with a staircase at the back behind the counter leading upwards to what Val knew was a studio flat that Brock's father used as an office and his mother used as a craft centre.

It had always amazed Val that the shop was entirely handmade by Brock's father. The rich mahogany had been cut, carved, and polished all by hand, as well as all sorts of steps that Val would never know to turn a hunk of wood into something so useful and beautiful. The front of the counter was decorated with a gorgeous natural landscape, flowers blooming around a large oak tree. Val knew it was based on one of Brock's child drawings, a picture he had drawn over and over as a phase when he was first learning. It had been put in on the tenth anniversary of the murders as a tribute to him. It was still lovingly looked after.

"Valkyrie Ellis!" Mr Walker boomed from his place behind the counter, placing his pen down gently between the pages of his trivia book. He pushed his glasses up his nose, thin wired frames that always gleamed under the bright lights. "What are we making this week, hm?"

"Dad wants a new desk," Val called with a smile. She may not have been crafty or very good at DIY, but she always felt at home when she was here with Mr Walker.

He and his son both shared a smile that could put her at ease in seconds and while Brock was already a good head taller than his father at eighteen forever, Mr Walker was bulkier. His blonde hair was thinning but his eyes twinkled as he approached her spot by the house numbers.

"From scratch again?" Mr Walker checked softly with a soft chuckle. "Got nothing left from the last project?"

"Ya know us. Always want to be overprepared." Val responded and then turned to look at the shelf behind her at a vast selection of nails.

"He looks sick, check if he's sick," Brock whispered from behind her. "He never wears a coat: he always says his scarf will be enough."

Val couldn't exactly blurt out or demand to know if Mr Walker was sick or even feeling under the weather. It would be rude, most of all, and second of all, it would be completely out of the field as Mr Walker instead asked her about the project.

Val had picked up enough on her previous visits to know which answers to ponder over so she may need to come back for another visit and which ones to answer immediately.

Val tapped the side of her leg four times in quick succession. *Not now.* Brock scowled at her but didn't interrupt his father, a habit that had not been broken over the decades. Mr Walker often told Val to call him Hugh, but she never did.

There was something about him that just commanded respect, not that he had ever demanded it. Perhaps that was why- Hugh Walker had spent years in retail and therefore he had the patience of a saint. He had seen every type of person come through those doors and he had come through every encounter with a smile on his face, ready for it to happen again.

As Mr Walker talked her through tips and the best things to use to create this desk that she never intended to build,

Val did manage to comment that the weather was quite warm for February although everyone seemed to be coming down with a horrible cold.

When Mr Walker responded that he and his wife had been lucky and neither of them had caught anything yet, Brock visibly relaxed. Brock paced around the pair in a constant circle, watching his father's every move as if he had to recreate every single twitch and tut himself later on.

"So, Valentine's Day yesterday." Mr Walker raised his eyebrows at her playfully as he helped her carry the items to the counter. Brock's frantic pacing slowed, and he stayed a few feet away from his tribute as if being within an arm's reach of it would burn him. "Did you have any plans?"

"I went on a date," Val admitted with a coy smile as she settled packets of nails and a brand-new hammer down next to the other items. Mr Walker made an interesting sound and Val carried on quickly. "What about you and Mrs Walker? Did you two do anything?"

Mr Walker waved the question off. "Almost thirty years of marriage: we have had enough of exciting Valentines. Add some candles to the dinner and go shopping for the discounted chocolate the next morning and that works for us."

"Except the year you knocked over the candle." Brock blurted out as he stared just above his father, at the photo of himself hanging on the wall in a handmade and hand-decorated frame. It was of Brock just as he looked now, without the wound. The sun was shining, and Brock was grinning wickedly straight into the camera. He looked like he had just been caught finishing up a laugh. "Mum started shrieking and panicking. Ruined the lace tablecloth she had just finished making and got wax all over her chicken. She made you promise no more candles on the table ever again."

Mr Walker didn't so much as twitch as Brock took his trip down memory lane, but Val couldn't help but glance over at him. She thought that maybe it was best that Brock's father couldn't see his son. The heartbreak on Brock's face was raw and his jaw was so clenched that Val would have been worried he would break it if that were possible.

Mr Walker bagged up each item as he scanned them, leaving Val to awkwardly clutch at her card and watch him. "Discounted chocolate is always a good plan." She agreed as he scanned the final item. Mr Walker chuckled in agreement as Val tapped her card and took the bag with a smile.

"Well, I'm glad you had a good one this year. Let me know if your dad wants any tips for this desk okay?" Mr Walker told her, and Val let out a genuine chuckle at that.

"I'm glad Mrs Walker finally forgave you for her table-cloth. Enough to light some candles again at least." Val joked as she slid her card into her pocket. "And I'll let my dad know. Thanks again, Mr Walker." Val gave him a little wave as she headed back down the aisle. She would go and sit in the car and pretend to be doing something until Brock was ready to come out with her. If he took over five minutes, then she knew to just drive home.

Brock was right on her heels, however, actually stepping into them every few steps as if he couldn't wait for her to move out of the door. "Why would you say that?" Brock hissed at her as she slid into the driver's seat. "I mean the look on his face- "

"What? He said about telling dad if he needs help! Although I thought by now, Brock, you would have realised that we aren't building the thing." Val put the bag on the backseat and turned to look at her friend, pretending to struggle with her safety belt as she did so.

"The candle comment, Valkyrie."

"Don't call me that." Val snapped her belt into place and then had 'trouble' getting her keys out of her pocket. "…. I didn't even realise. He'll probably think he mentioned it once. People do that you know, fill in the blanks with their own assumptions."

"So, you want him to think he's going mad? How charming of you."

"Don't be so dramatic. We both know this won't be what sets him off." Val purposely looked Brock in the eyes. They were filled with worry and anger and…fear. "Look, I'm sorry. I am. I wasn't thinking. But he'll be fine, and he'll fill that little blank up with some excuse like your mother told me it once and he'll be okay."

Brock didn't respond to that; he just turned his face away to look at the road. Val sighed softly before starting the drive home. Once they arrived back at the house, Jess had set up a large bowl of buttery popcorn, packs of candy, and a few cans of soda onto the living room table. A movie was already loaded up and ready.

"I thought we could have a movie day!" Jess beamed. She was sat on the bottom of the indoor stairs, exactly where she had stood when the two had left that morning. It was as if she had set the living room up and then come straight back to the stairs to watch the door and wait for them. "I know, I know, we were just at the movies last night, but it was so fun, right? You could even see if James is free later and we could all hang out together again. I like him, even if he can't see me."

Val and Brock exchanged a quick look as Jess hopped up from her seat and headed into the kitchen as she babbled about how fun last night was and did Val want a hot chocolate? It was so cold outside- yeah she'll just make Val a hot chocolate and then they could start the movie.

"She's losing it," Brock whispered into Val's ear, his eyes focused on the doorway to the kitchen as if Satan himself were going to walk back out. "We saw someone last night and…. well, I think I'm making it better."

Val had to stop herself from raising an eyebrow at that. Brock was always quick to anger or upset and he got over it quickly as well, but Jess was so rare to upset it was unnerving. The girl ghost had little moments of anger, but she always had them with a smile on her face.

Val had often privately thought that Jess was as close to an angel as anyone could get and that maybe she was different from Brock and Claire and all the other ghosts she had ever known. That idea had shattered over the past twenty-four hours. Jess was just as tormented, as upset and pained as the others. Val's heart gave a sharp twist.

"She's not losing it. She's human. She's upset and we are going to watch movies with her until she isn't," Val muttered back, and her face quickly twisted into a smile as Jess popped her head back in to tell Val she had found some marshmallows. "Sounds great. Thanks, Jess," she'd told the girl quickly and Jess shot her a thumbs up before heading back to the kitchen.

"Whatever you say." Brock rolled his eyes and threw himself back against the couch, tapping his legs to try and coax Oz from his place on the armchair and over to him. The dog trotted over happily, tongue lounging out of his mouth as it went straight past its owner to the ghost next to her instead.

"So," Jess chirped when she came back into the room, carefully placing a large mug with an overflowing amount of marshmallows and whipped cream onto a coaster on the glass table in front of them all. "Did you want to invite James? I think with a little bit of practise we could even make it so it's like a group thing!"

"Um," Val cleared her throat and reached over for the mug to buy some time for her response. While she would love to see James again after their date last night, Jess wanted something that wasn't going to happen. Val couldn't out-right interact with them in front of him and James couldn't see or hear them. They would just be left out of the conversation until James went home. Val took a sip of the drink and turned her head to look at Jess with some excuse, but her eyes were so hopeful and her lips into a soft smile, so Val blurted out "I'll check with him, okay?"

Brock shot her a look from behind Jess's head as the gorgeous brunette leaned over and gave Val a gentle squeeze. Oz gave a little whine as Brock had apparently stopped his strokes and Jess spun herself back around to focus on Oz as well. Val shot Brock a slight scowl before reaching for her phone and hovering her thumbs over the keyboard.

The date last night had ended well- remarkably well in Val's eyes. The two had laughed at the same parts of the horror movies, James' arm had made its way over her shoulder by the climax of the first movie and the night had ended with a kiss so soft and gentle Val had thought she was imagining it until she had felt his hand move up to caress her cheek.

It was a movie kiss, Jess had joked, and now Val was sitting here feeling like they were currently at the awkward part of a rom-com, where the girl had a secret that was going to ruin it all. She only wished that the secret was something more cliché, like she was moving away or dying.

Val had simply typed out the word 'hi' and then got stuck on how to open up the invitation to come over. Val saw three little dots in a bubble pop up on James' side of the screen and her heart gave a little flip. She forgot that was a feature. God, he must think she was typing out something insane or long or insanely long. It made it ten times worse trying to ask him now.

The bubble disappeared and then reappeared, and it looked like the two were in an awkward standoff of who would send their message first. Val had decided to just add on a blunt 'Having another movie night if you want to come over' and she pressed send just as she received James's message asking her if she was doing anything later. He then quickly sent her three laughing emojis as he realised what they had both been doing.

Val's phone gave another quick buzz as he followed his emojis with another message. *Are movies going to be our love language? I have some stuff to do but I can be at yours in a couple of hours. I'll message you when I'm on my way.*

Val typed back that it sounded like a plan and then slide her phone onto the table again. Jess was still stroking Oz while Brock gently fiddled with his fluffy ears. Oz looked like he was in heaven. "James is going to come over in a couple of hours," Val informed them softly and Jess turned her head so that Val could see her thankful smile.

"I like him. He's good for you. Brings you out of your shell and you need that. It's going to help you grow when you go to college. You're going to be so great at college, Val, you are." Jess never stopped her stroking of Oz, but her tone caught Val off-guard. It sounded like a goodbye. Brock seemed to have noticed it too and he moved his hand to catch Jess and squeezed it.

"Course she is. We'll be going with her and now, she'll know to listen to us so we can make her super popular." Brock shot Val a playful wink. "Can't help with the tests or anything but it's college; no one turns up to class anyway."

"It's Harvard. I'm pretty sure people go to class." Val frowned. "And if not, then I'm gonna have some lovely quiet lectures."

The conversation continued like that for well over the first half of the first movie. They argued about frat parties and Boston nightlife and no, Val, you're not going to be spending your first weekend at college finding the best spot at the library! The trio laughed and poked fun at each other, lounging against each other as much as they could but Val constantly felt an underlying tension. She wasn't sure if it was just her that was feeling it or she was imagining the forced happiness in Jess's eyes, but there was an unsaid thought drifting around with each mention of college- *They never got to go.*

Brock and Jess were having a playfully heated debate about if Val should join a society or not, getting louder and louder as they spoke over the other and Val laughing along with that she barely heard the doorbell. The only way she was sure it had even gone off was Oz leaping from his spot and trotting over to the door. She glanced over at her phone as she followed him. James hadn't messaged her or if he had then she had missed it.

Oz curled himself up at the side of the door, waiting with a wagging tail for Val to open the door. Val threw the door open, face set in a grin that slowly fell into a small confused smile as she caught sight of not James, but Mrs Walker.

Chapter Eight

Brock's mother was short and curvy with dirty blonde hair that bordered on brown, a cut into a sharp bob. She had been aged prematurely by stress and tragedy but there were laugh lines up by her eyes. She didn't look happy right now though. She looked somewhat terrified and awkward, and she was wringing her hands together until she caught sight of Val.

"Hi, Mrs Walker." Val greeted her awkwardly as she leaned against the door. "Are you okay?" Val knew that probably sounded ruder than asking if she could help or if something had happened, but the woman looked as if she was about to face off with some terrifying beast. Her face went even whiter as she locked eyes with Val.

"You talk to him, don't you?" The woman blurted out instantly and that starter point, that simple question, began a tirade. "My son. You talk to him. Not like all those sham women and mediums I went to; you can actually do it."

Val's heart started to beat so loud that she could have sworn Mrs Walker could hear it. The sound was echoing around in her eardrums, and she started to take some deep breaths, but they got caught in her throat as she tried to speak to explain or laugh away the accusation, but Mrs Walker was still going.

"You drift off. You talk to yourself at school but it's not yourself, is it? Kids at school just think it is. There are all sorts of rumours about you and when you're in the shop you either look at Brock's picture constantly or you make a point not to. You know things about our family that you shouldn't, that I didn't even tell those psychics with all their tarot cards. You had no way to know about our table-cloth." Mrs Walker was also taking deep breaths now but that was simply because she was talking so fast she was running out of oxygen between words.

Val once again opened her mouth to deny it, to gently tell this poor woman that she was sorry but no, she barely knew who Brock was, but that lie got stuck on her tongue. She refused to let herself say it. Mrs Walker probably wouldn't believe it either.

Her hands were now down at her sides, steady and calm and her eyes had a light behind them that Brock had every time he made a decision. Mrs Walker wasn't going away. Val pushed the door open to make way for her. "Do you want to come in?"

Mrs Walker stopped abruptly and then stared at her for a long second before stepping into the house. She looked around awkwardly and opened her mouth and then closed it again. Oz gave a small whine and then leant up to tap his nose against the woman's hand.

Val shut the door with a soft thud and turned to see Brock blocking the doorway into the living room, staring at his mother in absolute horror. Mrs Walker gave Oz a gentle pat on the head, oblivious to the fact her son was within arm's reach again.

"Maybe we should go in the living room," Val suggested softly and gestured with her hand towards where the women should go. Mrs Walker gave an awkward nod and moved slowly, as if all the energy had already left her.

Mrs Walker stopped briefly to look at the table, at the snacks and the still running movie screen. She gently licked her lips and opened her mouth again as if to apologise for intruding but once again stopped herself. Val smiled in a way that she hoped was reassuring and perched herself on the armrest of the couch.

Mrs Walker settled herself on the edge of a cushion on the other end. There was a heavy silence as Jess and Brock slowly traipsed into the room after them, the dead teenage boy moving at a snail's pace as if the room was going to burn him alive if he stayed in it so long.

"So," Val began awkwardly and cleared her throat. "I ...I can talk to ghosts." The sentence sounded so blunt and awkward coming out of her mouth and she realised that she had never said it so directly, out loud anyway. When she first talked to her father about it, he referred to it as their gift and that they could see people that others couldn't. The G-word was rarely said out loud. Mrs Walker released a breath that sounded somewhat relieved, so Val continued.

"I can see them as well. I've been able to for.... well, my whole life I guess. As long back as I can remember remembering." Val's tongue felt heavy in her mouth and everything she was saying sounded wrong, but she didn't know how else to explain it and now that she was saying it out loud, she couldn't stop.

"I met Brock at the high school. He's kinda hung around ever since. He talks about you a lot and I go to the shop so I can check-in and he has someone to go with him. Before I arrived, he stayed at yours and watched you and it....it broke his heart."

Val wanted to answer any questions the mother might have but she couldn't imagine her pain or where her mind would be, so she was undoubtedly missing a few. Tears were already pooling in Mrs Walker's eyes.

"Tell her I'm here." Brock choked out from his space hidden away in the corner of the room, as if he were a scolded child. His voice broke and his eyes were solely focused on his mother. "Wait for no... just...just tell her this is me. So, she knows where to look." Brock frantically reached for something to wave around and settled on a worn paperback from the bookshelves behind him.

"Don't be scared." Val had time to blurt out as Brock started to frantically wave the book about in the air. "He just...he wants you to see him too."

It would have been almost comical, the way Brock was moving, in wild arm gestures and lunges, making the book move around as much as physically possible to get his mother's attention if the Walkers' faces weren't so desperate and pained. Mrs Walker didn't look as if she were even breathing as her eyes moved around, intensely focussed on the cover of *The Warded Man* as if it held all the answers to the universe.

"My Boy." Mrs Walker choked out before bursting into sobs. She cupped her face into her hands as the tears flowed free and fast down her face. "Oh, my baby boy."

"Mommy." Brock stopped moving the book and dropped to his knees in front of her, right in the middle of the table as if it wasn't even there. Val knew from Jess that it was an incredibly uncomfortable thing to do, but Brock simply hovered his free hand over his mother's as if it would pull it away and take it.

"If you feel something cold, it's him," Val whispered. "Whenever you feel a cold spot, it's him. He can't touch you properly. It will just feel like a cold, vague shape but it's him. He's right in front of you."

Mrs Walker turned her head to look at Val for a second, eyes red and searching to see if this were all some cruel joke, but a floating book was pretty hard to explain away under a surprise visit. She turned back and looked straight in front of her. She quickly, as if she were going to change her mind, snapped her palms out in front of her. She went straight through Brock's forehead. Brock couldn't help himself, he let out a teary chuckle. "Your aim was always terrible," Brock whispered. "Didn't matter what it was for, you always missed." Brock then reached out and gently rested his hands on her arms.

Mrs Walker let out a gentle gasp and then started to cry again. "I can feel him. Oh, I can- Brock Walker, you hug me right this second!" Brock happily obliged and Val wished she had a ghost-friendly camera that would pick this up, for Mrs Walker and for Brock. The two were clinging to each other as if it was the end of the world. Val supposed that for them, that had already happened.

Mrs Walker was sobbing uncontrollably only a few seconds later and Val went to reach for her but stopped awkwardly halfway across the sofa. Jess had disappeared somewhere or simply gone invisible for the time being. Val couldn't blame her; this was a rough sight for Val, and it would hit Jess ten times harder. Jess would probably never have this moment with her mother, and she had spent decades with Brock. They had died together. They were as close as two people could possibly be.

Mrs Walker settled herself back against the cushions and stared in front of her, eyes still streaming tears and a bright red. "My baby." She whispered, "Oh my baby.....you've been here all this time. All this time."

Brock nodded as if his mother could see and then he stilled, turning his head to look at Val who answered for him with a soft, "Yes." Mrs Walker also looked at her then and she reached out to clasp at her hand.

"Is he happy? Is he okay? He's not- was he in- he must have been so scared. In so much pain." Mrs Walker's voice gave a hitch and Val's heart shot up into her throat as she realised she was asking about Brock's final moments. Brock had never told her about them in detail, only vague references, or details that she could have found in old newspaper articles.

"Tell her no," Brock begged Val immediately. "Tell her I'm happy now. That I was okay. She won't believe you so just.... tell her I was too cold to notice. She already knows it wasn't quick so don't say that."

Val swallowed a few times to try and clear the lump in her throat, the back of her eyes pricking as she held back her tears at that. "He says he's happy now and that he was okay. That he was too cold to notice the pain." Val looked down at their hands, then as Mrs Walker let out a strangled noise, and clutched at her hand.

Val squeezed her hand back and immediately regretted what she had said. She should have lied, told her that he hadn't felt anything due to the shock. The truth hadn't helped, and Mrs Walker hadn't waited over twenty years only to be told that Brock was cold, bleeding out in the school hallway and shivering. She hadn't wanted that. She wanted to be told that Brock was happy and-

"Loved." Val blurted out. "You should know that he is very loved here. I adore him. He's the best person I've ever met. You raised him amazingly. You should be incredibly proud."

Brock was staring at Val as if she had shed her skin and his mother was looking at her with a sad watery smile. "Was he alone all this time? Just waiting for you?"

Val hesitated for a second and then shook her head. It wasn't her place to say which of the other kids had stuck around, to tell Brock's mother exactly whose children had also been stuck on this side of paradise. "A few of the kids stuck around. He's always had people." Val had never thought about it that way, that Jess and Brock had just been waiting around for someone like Val to come along.

Val had always thought about it as just another reminder she was abnormal and finding a way to make it work. She quickly decided she preferred to think about it as Mrs Walker did, that this was fate. She and Brock were destined to end up best friends, to spend Val's high school days reminiscing over his high school interests and blurring the lines of reality a little at a time.

Mrs Walker released a breath and nodded her head slowly. She looked relieved at that. Her face was soaked, and her eyes were bloodshot but the sadness that always seemed etched into her face every time Val had seen her before seemed to have lessened although it would never fade completely.

"I'm sorry for barging in as this," Mrs Walker apologised in a broken whisper. "I just, when I started to think about it all and I pieced it together, I ...I couldn't get it out of my mind. It was driving me insane. I just wanted you to tell me I was crazy and send me home, remind me again that I'm a silly old woman that couldn't let go."

"You're not a silly old woman. You're a good mother who missed her child who never should have been taken from you in the first place." Val reassured her. This conversation was becoming more honest than she had expected when she first opened up the door. The air was thick with it, a different sort of tension than before. Val knew that whatever she would say, whatever Mrs Walker would admit, it would be accepted.

"You never gave up." Val continued. "You never gave up on him. That's all we could ever really hope for as people. For someone to love us that much that they refuse to let us go. I don't think Brock would have made it all these years if you hadn't kept believing."

"Damn straight I wouldn't," Brock agreed quickly and ran his hand over his mother's arm.

"Brock agrees." Val's lips tilted into a smile and Mrs Walker was looking in her son's vague direction, Brock constantly moving his arm so that his mother knew where he was based on the cold spot. Val pressed her lips together to stop from smiling even wider at the image.

"Brock," Val said slowly, and the boy looked over at her with wide eyes, "you can hold things. You can write things... why don't you take your mother upstairs or go with her. Spend some time. You can write your part of the conversations down. Maybe even convince your dad."

Val didn't want it to seem like she was pushing Mrs Walker out the door or throwing Brock into a situation that he wasn't ready for, but she was hyperaware that she was acting as a moderator here and that Mrs Walker and Brock might just prefer for this to be a little more private. They didn't have to worry about Mrs Walker seeing random floating objects after all and now she had figured it out, it was likely that Mr Walker had already been told about her theory. There was no point in the secret anymore, not for them.

"I would like that." Mrs Walker admitted. "If Brock wants- if you want to." Mrs Walker turned her head once again in Brock's vague direction. Brock shot Val a toothy smile before hopping up and looking around for a pen and paper. Val leaned forward and started rooting through the shelf underneath the glass table. She grabbed the first notebook she found and handed it over to him. Mrs Walker let out an amazing breath as the notebook seemingly hovered in mid-air and then moved as if it were tucked underneath an arm.

"That's a yes," Val told her softly, "although I can't see a pen..."

"I have a pen." Mrs Walker said as she threw herself to her feet. "I have many pens. That's, that's just fine." Mrs Walker kept her eyes focussed on the notebook even as she adjusted her jumper. Val nodded at her, smiling widening as she caught sight of how Brock seemed to shine under his mother's gaze.

"Thank you, Val," Brock whispered to her as he lunged forward and wrapped his arm around her in a tight hug on his way to the door. He was moving faster than he usually did, already moving towards the door as if he was a child late for a school field trip. Mrs Walker's eyes were going wild as they followed the notebook, but she stopped to pull Val into a bone-crushing hug.

"I'll never be able to thank you enough for this." The woman whispered. "If you ever need anything, you come straight to me. Anything. You've given me my heart back."

The woman let her go and immediately looked around for the notebook. Val turned her head as well and saw Brock fidgeting in the hallway.

"He's excited." Val breathed and gave Mrs Walker's arm a gentle squeeze. "And happy. That's all I care about." The two then shared a smile before Mrs Walker headed towards the door. Val held it together all of ten seconds after hearing the front door close before bursting into tears.

Jess still didn't reappear even as Val sobbed in Oz's fur on the sofa. The movie had played itself out and her hot chocolate was long cold. The whipped cream dribbled down the sides as it had melted, and it was only as Oz tried to start licking it off of the table that Val pulled herself together and pushed herself to her feet. She focussed on cleaning the table and topping up Oz's water and on not thinking about Brock and his parents that it was all she could think about.

She could just imagine Brock sat there at a handmade dining room table, writing his responses thoughtfully across lines of the notebook, sticking his tongue slightly out like he did when trying hard to make something look presentable. Mrs Walker watching the pen move with wide eyes. Mr Walker goes silent as the blank page fills up with his son's handwriting.

Three loud raps on the front door had Val jumping, throwing the hot chocolate covered cloth into the sink as she ran to get it. Brock would be able to just materialise in the house again, but Mrs Walker couldn't and maybe she had forgotten something-

For the first time, Val opened the door and was disappointed to see James. Val felt her smile drop and then quickly put one on. James noticed however and his smile faded. "You didn't get my message," James stated, "and you've been crying. You like watching sad movies alone?"

"Something like that," Val agreed lamely and opened up the door wide enough for him to come in. James stepped inside and Val noticed he was carrying a carrier bag branded from the local stop and go. "Sorry I didn't notice the message. Oz had at my hot chocolate, so I was cleaning that up," Val lied as she shut the door behind him.

"He didn't drink any, did he?" James asked and looked over at her with worried eyes.

"No, no he'll be fine. It just spilt on the table and.... anyway. What kind of movie are you thinking of? Your choice." Val offered with a fake brightness. "Well, okay nothing sad."

James turned and looked at her, head slightly tilted, and his lips pressed together as he took her in. "Sit down. I'll make you another hot chocolate. You look frazzled. Was it a horror movie or something?" James' voice was gentle but that put Val more on edge than before.

She had watched her dead best friend reunite with his grieving mother after being confronted about a gift she had tried to keep to herself for eighteen years that she had then revealed, and Jess wasn't here to talk to. She felt like she was a balloon that had been overinflated, one wrong poke away from exploding. That poke could be anything and she knew it. Everything could be a trigger that sent her spiralling into another crying fit or blurting her secret out to James.

He would think she was insane, metal, loopy, and he would be out that door faster than Brock had been. He would leave her in the best-case scenario and the worst case he would post on his socials that they broke up because she had decided she could see ghosts. It would spread and Harvard would be snatched away from her as well. It would follow her everywhere she went just like she had always feared.

"No really, I'm good," Val told him quickly, "I just, it got me. I don't even know why I just kinda started crying at it." Val settled herself into the corner of the sofa. She could play it off like that, that some random movie was surprisingly emotional. She could last a few hours doing that until he went home and then she could break down again in private.

As soon as she finished that thought, Claire Rickard appeared in the middle of the room, screaming like a banshee, and causing the lights to flicker uncontrollably. Val barely had time to breathe before a hardback was flying through the air straight at her head.

Chapter Nine

"Brock got to speak to his MOTHER," Claire howled, grabbing another book from the shelves, and throwing it at Val again as soon as she saw that the girl had ducked away from the last one. The lights were flashing on and off so fast that Val thought she was at a rave rather than her worst nightmare.

James was stood, looking wildly up at the lights and then at the floating books. He had dropped the bag and now soda was slowly pumping out of burst cans all over the carpet. That was the sight that had Val clenching her fists and jumping to her feet.

"CLAIRE." Val boomed. "Enough! You're not a god damn toddler." She was aware that to James, she was speaking to nothing but then that also meant that *nothing* was throwing books at her. She at least wouldn't look crazy, although she fully expected to get dumped and for him to still run. Her stomach flared up with a white-hot feeling of rage at the thought that the boy she loved was going to be run out of the house by Claire flipping Rickard.

Claire's face was no longer beautiful. It was contorted into a gross twist of betrayal and rage. "How dare you." Claire snarled, and she held up yet another book to throw. "How dare you do that for only one of us you vile little- "

"I didn't realise you came as a group. You never have before," Val snapped, and she prepared herself to lunge to the side or duck if the book started coming her way. "And how dare *I*? How dare you? Come in here, start wrecking the place in front of other people. You've always been bitchy, Claire, but this takes the cake."

"Oh, I'm so sorry I ruined your little date night with my grieving." Claire took a step forward. "I'm so sorry I'm upset because Brock got his PARENTS BACK." She threw the book then and Val dropped down to avoid it as Claire carried on. "It's ridiculous, really. I should have put a stop to this back when you first turned up here, but Jess liked you, said you were nice." Claire scoffed, just as James scrambled to Val's side and grabbed her hand.

Val kept her eyes straight ahead on Claire in case she decided to grab something else. James had taken the lack of flying objects as a good sign, although the lights were still flickering to the point where Val was afraid the bulbs were going to explode on them.

"We need to get out of here," James told her in a fierce whisper, and he looked up at the lights. He gently but firmly pulled her to her feet and started towards the door, but Val yanked her arm back. She would not, she absolutely would *not* be run from her home because of a dead girl's tantrum.

"Come on then," Val growled, and she even made a beckoning gesture at her. "Come and put a stop to this now. But I'm gonna come back and haunt you right back you selfish egotistic hypocritical bitch. You're the reason Brock and Jess are dead in the first place." Val took a step around the table then as Claire flinched away as if Val had thrown something back at her.

James, to his credit, had stayed in the same spot. Val could feel his eyes on her but didn't dare break the staring contest she had going on with Claire. Val kept advancing and Claire slowly moved backwards around the room to keep the same distance between them.

"You bullied that kid. You pushed and pushed and pushed at him until he broke. Jess was only there to help you with your hair for a photo shoot for your prom campaign. It went completely against her own, but she did it because you were her friend. Brock was only there to help you get all the stuff back home. They were doing YOU a favour and they died for it. Now you have the absolute nerve- the god damn *audacity* to come into my home and attack me because Brock got something you wanted?" Val took a giant step forward then and closed the gap between the girls.

"Get the hell out of my house.," Val whispered. "And if I ever see you back here, I'll go to your grave, dig you up, and salt and burn you. If that doesn't work? I'll try every single thing the internet tells me to until you're nothing."

Claire looked at Val and blinked once. Her eyes were wide, and they looked like they were pooling with tears. Claire's bottom lip even wobbled slightly, although it looked as if she were clenching her jaw. She didn't say another word, just vanished with a slight sniff.

Once she was gone, Val released a long breath, which was interrupted by James blurting out, "Did you just threaten the ghost that haunts your house?" Val didn't answer him for a second, instead leaning down to pick up the spilt cans.

The soda had soaked in and while she knew she should turn and console James and explain, coming up with an excuse or explanation that wouldn't lead to another argument. But she was exhausted from the last few hours alone, but she still needed to walk Oz and she wanted to wait for Brock and –

"She doesn't haunt the house. She doesn't even like me." Val sighed as she started to try and clean up the mess. "She doesn't now. I can.... I can explain, just let me clean this up first." Val practically ran to the kitchen to grab something to dab at the soda with, taking a few deep breaths before going back to the living room.

She was two steps in, maybe three, before she stopped. James had started to tidy up all the books that had been thrown at her, sliding them back into the empty spots in the bookcase. He turned his head to look at her and shot her a nervous half-smile.

Please don't leave me, Val thought instantly and then awkwardly headed over to the spill. *Dear God, please don't leave me.* Val knew that was pathetic and potentially selfish. If he stayed, he would be stuck here with her in her weirdo bubble, forever stuck with the knowledge that things did go bump in the night, people did get stuck after death and had to watch their loved one's age and their only company is other dead people unless they stumbled across a freak like her.

Eventually, there was no more cleaning to do and the two ended up standing at opposite ends of the room staring at each other and unsure of how to proceed.

"You must have loads of questions," Val said softly and started to play with her fingernails as she stared at him. "Do you...do you wanna sit or did you wanna leave and take some time? Or we could, um, we could go for a walk. I need to take Oz out at some point so..."

"Who's Brock? And Jess? You mentioned them when you were yelling at.... whomever you were yelling at," James asked immediately, and he stood there for a second before slowly setting himself down in the armchair in the corner of the room. Val awkwardly perched herself on the edge of a couch cushion as far as she could be from him. If he wanted space from her while this was settled, then she could understand that.

"Brock Walker and Jess Poole," Val answered. "Brock's parents own and run the DIY store. Jess's mum works as a hairdresser." Val could see that James recognised the walker's names, or was at least aware of them, but was confused. She supposed that was to be expected so she carried on explaining.

"They were victims of a school shooter back in April 1998. A group of kids were helping Claire with her prom queen campaign." Val cleared her throat and looked down. "Brock was the first. He was shot in the chest; it got his lungs. He bled out in the hall while Logan went into the classroom. Jess was shot in the neck. No one survived. Logan tried to shoot himself afterwards, but he just shifted by one of the people he shot. He ended up in hospital for a few days before succumbing to his injuries."

Val glanced up at James and found him nodding slowly. James caught her eye and once again smiled at her although this time it was barely there. "How long have you been able to see them?" Jess leant forward in the chair then, elbows on his knees and hands clasped under his jaw as he stared at her.

Val had expected another question about the school shooting, about the ghost that had been here throwing things, but that wasn't exactly an unexpected question either. She just thought that would be low on the priority list.

"I can't even remember," Val admitted, and her brow furrowed as she tried to remember her first-ever ghost. If she was going to lay everything bare to someone then she wanted it to be as accurate as possible. "The first one I remember knowing was a ghost was my friend's mum. She had cancer. I didn't even know she had died until her daughter started screaming at me, asking why I was being so mean. That her mum was gone and why was I saying I could see her. But my dad mentioned once that I kept saying I saw a man in my kindergarten class. A man no one else could."

Val cleared her throat and rubbed her hands together. "Brock and Jess I met my first day at school after I moved. My parents looked into the area and couldn't find anything major online, so they thought this place was a safe bet." Val rolled her eyes at that. "Apparently no one thought to upload anything about the school shooting to the internet. Very helpful of them."

"When you shouted in class." James realised, and his tone was almost excited. "That was at one of them. When you look like you're staring at nothing or when you do that cute little chuckle under your breath. I always thought you were just two steps ahead of us on it all. That the teachers or your lab partner had just said something funny, and they hadn't even realised it. But it was Brock or Jess, wasn't it?"

Val nodded her confirmation and her face automatically lifted into a smile. "Brock usually. Jess likes to pay attention in class or at least get me to pay attention, so my grades don't look so sketchy. Brock argues that since they give me the answers to the tests, I don't need to pay attention anyway." Val leant back into the sofa and crossed her arms. "They aren't here right now if you were wondering. Brock's mum figured it out, what I could do, and she came over and...Brock's over with his parents right now. Jess disappeared during the reunion. It was hard for her." Val added quickly just so there was no confusion about the fact that the ghosts had feelings and Val didn't blame her, not one single bit.

James let out a breezy half-laugh that confused Val. James caught her look and explained quickly "It's just...I always thought you being alone all the time was because you didn't really need anyone. That you were just happy with yourself. But you've never been alone, have you?"

"I suppose not." Val agreed slowly but James was still going.

"You've kept this secret all this time. All those times people have called you names and belittled you and you never even blinked. You're so special and you just sit there and take it. You're telling me your ghost friends couldn't have taken some sweet revenge for you?" James tilted his head to try and catch Val's eye. She had gone slightly red at the fact he had called her special and the fact he hadn't bolted out of the back door. Val shook her head at him and went to explain but that wasn't necessary.

"You tell them not to, don't you?" James realised "Otherwise my friends would have long since been beaten up. They are ghosts: it's not like there would be any consequences for them."

Val laughed then. "Brock offered once. I told him if he laid even a finger on a living person, I would ignore him for the rest of my existence. I could handle high school without a nineties football player going vigilante on some scumbags that think I should be on crazy pills."

"You constantly have a football player hanging around and offering to beat people up for you?" James raised his eyebrows at her. "Should I be jealous?"

Val shot him an unamused look but then laughed. Her stomach was lurching and wiggling around as she looked at him like something was about to burst from it. He didn't even look scared, barely confused anymore, and his eyes were trying to catch hers. It was the complete opposite of what she had expected. "You're not gonna break up with me? I'm…. seriously freaky confirmed now." Val wanted it to come out nonchalant as if this was a situation that she had played out before.

James, however, looked startled and sat back in his chair as if that question had knocked the wind from him. "Valkyrie Ellis I'm tempted to kiss you right now because of how *seriously freaky* you think you are," James told her quickly, words stumbling over each other. "You've never complained, not really, about what you get put through at school. You smile as if there's nothing that could get you to stop and now you face down and threaten a ghost, your best friends are dead, and you're sat here staring at me with those big, beautiful eyes still insulting yourself."

James said it all in a quick ramble as if he was suddenly going to be cut off. His hands had gripped the side of the armchair as he did so and Val pushed herself to her feet, moving slowly towards him, having to make an awkward sidestep around Oz, who had settled himself exactly half-way in-between the two of them. James shifted as if to meet her halfway, but then changed his mind. He kept his eyes focused on her, even as she climbed into his lap and pressed her lips hard against his.

James' hand went immediately into her hair and his other onto her waist. Val was pulled as close as possible to him. She wasn't sure how she had gone from crying over Brock to making out with James on her mother's favourite chair, but as soon as his soft lips pushed her own open, all thoughts of Brock and her mother were gone.

All she could think about was how soft James' hair felt under her palms and how warm the rest of him was. It hadn't registered beforehand exactly how much colder a ghost was than a human. She had been so used to the cold spots of ghosts; Brock wrapping his arm around her and Jess's hugs. James embraces felt like sitting in a fireplace, but she didn't hate it.

"I love you."

James's confession had Val pulling back, hands still entangled in his silky black hair. James' eyes fluttered open and stared immediately into her own. "I love you," he repeated. "You don't have to say it back. I know that it's really, really fast but I do."

"I love you too," Val said as soon as he was finished. She didn't want to interrupt him-what would be more terrible than interrupting a love confession, but she didn't want him thinking his feelings were one-sided. Val could have only dreamt she would be in this position- actually no. She had never dreamt this one up exactly.

It was usually confessed over a cliché candlelit dinner, or a random thought said out loud while they were entangled together watching a movie. The occasional dream would involve a recreation of their first date, but never a make-out session after confessing she can see ghosts.

James' face broke into a wide grin that made Val feel better than a thousand sunny days. He looked relieved as if he hadn't been entirely sure of her reaction, so Val readjusted her hold on his hair and whispered "You are literal perfection, you know that? I have no idea why you're slumming it and loving me but whatever god I have to thank for it, I will make sure their sacrifice is worth it."

It was dry humour; however, James's face turned serious all of a sudden. Val realised that since she had just dumped on him that ghosts were real, the poor boy probably thought she could see celestial beings as well.

"I don't think gods are real," Val added quickly and leaned back even more. "And I've never seen a vampire or a werewolf. No witches, no wizards, or three-headed dogs. Just people that are a little covered in blood and stuck on this side of nothingness."

"Covered in blood?" James echoed with a frown. "You mean that they…. however, they died…"

Val gave a solemn little nod and James' nose screwed up. Val guessed that he was thinking of every way he had ever seen or heard about anyone dying. How their necks looked when they were twisted at a wrong angle, or how much blood pumped out from a stab wound. It would all be Hollywood-based (she hoped) but it would be close enough for him to realise exactly what she saw every day.

"Well, that explains why you have such a strong stomach." James rested his head against the back of the chair. "School shooter victims aren't exactly known for going peacefully."

Val flinched at that. She had imagined it over it and over, more so back when she had first met them. The idea of Jess's face screwed up and screaming for mercy had haunted her for a while, even though she knew it probably wasn't accurate. The idea of Brock fighting for his life and failing had her shuddering.

"Sorry," James said bashfully and tightened his hold on her. "That was insensitive. I just…. I would never be able to cope with that. I'm a wuss. Plus, everything I do gets put online and unless you can suddenly take photos with ghosts, that would be too big an obstacle for me." James' voice turned playful at the end, although Val knew that his social media was like a love letter to his life. Everything he enjoyed went on there. James paused then and struggled for a minute to dig his phone out of his pocket. Val had to shift to let him get it.

Once successful, his face was lit up as he unlocked it and then paused. "You said there's not a lot of stuff online about them? Your friends?" Val shook her head and then slowly peeled herself away from him to pad up the stairs.

Once in her room, she ducked under her bed and dragged out the small cardboard box. She gently removed the old yearbook but kept the rest of the stuff there. It was all a mix of things she had picked up from the local charity and thrift stores- gummy bracelets and a scrunchie that Jess swore she had matches of back in the day, a polaroid camera that Brock said he had always wanted but never got around to buying. The pride of place was the 1998 class yearbook in okay condition.

James was still in the armchair, rubbing his hands to-gether as he waited for Val to come back. Val was flicking through the pages as she walked across the room until she finally came across the memorial section.

Each victim got a double-page spread whereas the shooter was wiped from it completely. He wasn't in a single group shot. Everyone else's pages all had a large school ID photo and then a photo collage underneath that. The other page was full of quotes from their friends and teachers. The memorial pages were in alphabetical order, but Val stopped at Brock's first before handing the book over.

"This is Brock."

James stared down at the photos, holding the book as gently. "Definitely should be jealous," James whispered playfully, half-heartedly trying to break the tension. Val let out an amused breath through her nose. "Seriously." James told her "Even I know he's hot. Plus, according to this, he was 'pretty killer' in English, and you love English."

"I don't love English," Val muttered in her defence as she settled herself on the armrest of the chair so she could look at the pages at the same time. "I'm just.... good at it."

"You love English." James argued "Your face lights up every time you sit in that room. It's the complete opposite to what it does whenever you go into Spanish." James gently ran his fingers over each word on Brock's page. He made sure to read every single one and if Val hadn't said it earlier, she would have told him that she loved him right there.

Instead, she gently nudged her shoulder against his. "You're sounding like a stalker right now."

"A stalker you're in love with." James paused his reading to look up at her through his lashes. His smile turned shy then and he looked down at the page before admitting, "I've kind of been watching you for a while."

Val raised her eyebrows at him, but he carried on in a forced playful tone. "Not a little while. Since you moved. You've always just kinda been there and you were just different, and I thought that was so strange and then it went from that to think it was cute and then it was hot and then it went to literal prayers that you would notice when I spoke up in class and give me that amused little look you seemed to give thin air. I could have kissed Mr Hendricks in the middle of class when he paired us together."

James kept his head down and Val stared at him for a few seconds. James Rogers had been crushing on her for three years, by his admission. Val remembered that he had dated other people during that time.

His name was always floating around the school with some kind of adoring rumour or update, the opposite of what was said about her until he had publicly declared them an item. Now if her name was heard in the halls, it was about how lucky she was, how different she was now she had a boyfriend.

"That was very sweet." Val began slowly, and James' fingers once again stilled on the page. Val noticed it was under the quote from Brock's old girlfriend- *He was a total sweetheart. I'll never get over him. Rest in peace baby.*

James shrugged at that, and Val continued, "I remember when I first saw you. I was in the hall, very first morning, right before homeroom and I was struggling with my locker. I was so early that no one else was really in the hall but I hear this booming laugh. I thought it sounded better than anyone else's I had ever heard. I look over and it's you, in this classic white shirt black jacket combo. The sunlight is hitting the back of your head and it makes you look like your glowing. I've hidden away behind my locker door like some kind of creep. You walk right on past with Holly."

James slowly turned his head to the side and grinned at her. "We are both creepy, aren't we?"

"Well as long as it's creepy for each other," Val smirked, "then I think it's just romantic."

"Well as long as there's a way to twist it." James joked as he turned back to the memorial pages. Once he had reached the end of the page, Val slowly reached out and flipped over a few pages to get to Jess's. She stopped at Claire's for a not-so-honourable mention.

"That's the one I yelled at," Val told him in a mutter. "Ya know, if your mind was trying to fill in the blank there."

"Currently my mind is on the cute football player that gets to be around you literally every minute of every day." James smirked but he was looking at Claire's photos with a certain interest. "Although she looks...." James trailed off as if he was trying to think of a word that wouldn't be an insult. "Incredibly picturesque." He decided and then quickly explained. "There's not a hair out of place in a single photo. It's unnerving how camera-ready she must have been. Must have been."

"She's pretty intense about appearance." Val agreed and moved on to Jess's page. Jess's was one of her favourites. The quotes were all about her heart, how she had helped people through her few short years. There was no mention of how much potential had been wasted or how she would never see the Patriots win the Superbowl like there was on Brock's.

Her picture also included a family photo of her and her two little brothers outside the high school on their first day. Her smile, even in a twenty-year-old photo, shone like a sunbeam and while Val automatically smiled back, she was pleased to find that James was smiling as well.

"Now she...she looks the opposite. I mean she looks great but it's effortless. Are her and Claire enemies? I can totally see them being enemies."

"Nope," Val said softly, "friends."

"Nah." James shrugged as he gently pointed at Jess's smiling face. "That girl right there being friends with a perfectionist, tantrum-throwing cheerleader? I just can't see it."

"Seriously," Val insisted. "They are. Jess was helping Claire with her prom campaign, even though she was running as well. That's why she was still in school that day. She was collateral damage." Val's voice ended in a whisper and there was a silence that settled over the room like a cosey blanket. Val was nuzzled into James' side and their legs tangled with each other as they stayed in the armchair rather than move to the couch as James went through every single memorial page in that yearbook.

Chapter Ten

That was how Val's parents found them, stumbling through the door with their hands intertwined as if they were lovestruck teenagers. Val's mother was beaming at them, and James grinned back at her.

Val's father's face slipped from a smile to a slight frown as he realised what they were both looking at. He glanced over at his daughter, who was looking at her parents with a sheepish smile and flushed cheeks.

"He knows," Val confirmed, and her mother's smile flickered but kept steady.

"Brock?" Her mother guessed as she detangled herself from her husband and placed her jacket on the back of the sofa. "It was definitely Brock, right." Charlotte Ellis threw herself down onto the sofa, reaching her arm out to beckon over her dog as she shot her husband a triumphant grin. "It was totally Brock."

Val and James gave each other a confused look at that until Daniel dramatically sighed and settled in beside his wife. "I should know better by now," Daniel agreed, "taking bets against a detective. So.... was it Brock that spilt the beans?" Daniel turned his gaze over to James, who snorted.

"Brock's pretty important around here, huh?" He checked and Val hoped that James didn't see the pitying look that briefly flashed on her mother's face.

"He makes himself known," Charlotte agreed delicately. "I don't know what Val's told you about us, but even I can feel it when he's around. Not as much as Claire, but she only turns up once in a blue moon."

"She was my bet," Daniel cut in and put on a dramatic pout as his wife once again grinned at her victory.

"I hate to tell you this, Mrs Ellis," James said, "But....er....."

Daniel pressed his lips together to stop from laughing as his wife shook her head in disbelief. Her blonde wavey locks were covering her face she was shaking that much.

"Oh, damn it," she eventually sighed. "She ruins all my china and now this? She's the reason I hate cheerleaders."

"I know sweetie." Daniel reached over and gave her knee a gentle squeeze. "I know." Daniel shot James and Val a playful wink as his wife made a big deal of reaching in her jacket and grabbing her keys.

She then slowly undid a bashed-up, scratched-to-oblivion Pac-Man keychain. It was shaped like the Blinky the ghost, but the colours were faded from the years it had spent in pockets. She handed it over to her husband, who fist-bumped the air before frantically adding it to his keys.

"Your bet was a keychain?" James' brow was furrowed in confusion and Val shifted herself on his lap before quickly explaining.

"They went to an arcade for their first date. Wasted all of their money until they won only that keychain from a quarter machine. They've fought over who got to keep it ever since." Val had always thought the keychain was a perfect representation of her parent's relationship. That thing had lasted multiple decades, moves across the country, a daughter, police chases and long nights of emergency surgeries and had come out of all of it still looking pretty good.

"And I have proudly kept it for most of that time." Charlotte gave a playful sniff and tilted her head away from her husband, who gave his new keychain a little jiggle. The sound of the keys clanging against each other sent Val into a giggle and her father smiled over at her.

"What have I missed?" Brock declared, rubbing his hands together as he popped into the middle of the room. Brock was practically glowing almost to the point where Val thought he had gained a body. Brock's hand movements stopped as he caught sight of James. "Oh."

"Hello, Brock." Daniel greeted him softly and Brock looked at him as if he had just loudly announced he was leaving Charlotte to become a backup dancer for Beyonce. It took Brock only a second to realise what the greeting meant. When his head snapped to look over at Val, she simply smiled and pointed at him.

Brock shot her two-finger guns back as James took the hint and looked in the direction his girlfriend was pointing.

"It's nice to meet you." James gave an awkward one-handed wave while the other hand ran up and down Val's back. Val gave his shoulder a reassuring squeeze. When Brock didn't say anything, just crossed his arms and examined the pair like they were a painting in the louvre, Val lied and told James that he said hi.

"Don't put words into my mouth," Brock grumbled although he was on such a high from earlier that there was a constant smile on his face. Brock settled himself on the edge of the couch's armrest and rested his head lazily against the wall. Val rolled her eyes at him but said nothing.

The conversation with the rest of the group was mistimed but not awkward. Daniel and Val gave it their best shot at interacting with Brock and their partners but there were awkward gaps. James seemed not to notice, assuming that they were waiting on a ghost's response. Charlotte, who knew Brock well enough through her daughter, husband, and notes around the house, guessed that her family were purposely cutting out less desirable comments from Brock.

The conversation only twisted into awkward as Val's parents said their goodnights, kissing their daughter's forehead before leaving upstairs. Val heard her mother let out a distinct giggle once they thought they were out of earshot at the top of the stairs.

"Gross." Val and Brock said in unison and then both laughed. Val looked straight over at him as she did so and the fact she could do that without having to pretend it was at something else sent a thrill up her spine.

James and Val had moved themselves over to the couch, stretching their legs out after so long stuck on the chair. James looked over at her with an amused smile that flickered slightly as her gaze was elsewhere.

"We need to talk later." Brock leant towards her, whispering as if James could actually hear him. "When boy toy is gone. If you wanna hear about it that is."

"I wanna hear about it." Val reassured him "But you're right...later."

"Hear about what?" James asked Val softly, eyes flickering from her to the vague direction she had been looking at.

"Oh, you didn't tell him why I was missing today? Did I really just slip from your mind that easily?" Brock teased and gave her a gentle nudge with his shoulder. Val rolled her eyes before turning to look at James.

"How his reunion went with his dad," Val said softly and then added quickly, "but not while you're here, don't worry. Total inclusion. You're gonna be so involved in the chat you're gonna be hearing Brock's voice in your head for weeks."

"He can't hear my voice."

"Shut up, Brock." Val snapped back without even looking and James raised an eyebrow at her before leaning forward to gently kiss her cheek.

"I'll imagine him with a high squeaky...Elmo-like voice." James told her playfully.

"Watch it, pretty boy, or I'll take a page out of Claire's pink fluffy book and haunt your ass," Brock said.

Val reached over and swatted at his leg as she smiled at James. "Not quite but it's close enough," Val lied. "You're doing so well with this by the way. Amazing. If there was an award for boyfriends who could deal with their girlfriends living a secret life with supernatural beings, you'd be a front runner."

"And the presenter would have quite the mouthful to read." James quipped back, and Val giggled. James let out a small chuckle and gently reached out to tap her nose.

"Dear God, who do you people think you are, Romeo and Juliet?" Brock muttered.

"Romeo and Juliet both die, so hopefully not," Val shot back at Brock, although she kept her eyes on James. "He asked whom we thought we are, Romeo and Juliet?" Val echoed Brock's previous comment.

"I always preferred Hamlet," James said, peering his head around Val's to look at the empty seat and smiling. He was trying and that was all Val could ask and while Brock smiled back, the smile was like that of a toddler forced to sit with his least favourite cousin.

The rest of the evening flew by the same. Val echoing and editing Brock's comments to James, James trying hard to make friends with Brock and Brock playing nice but reserved. It was only when James' phone started buzzing uncontrollably and he could no longer ignore it that the night came to an end.

"It's Holly," James explained quickly as he unlocked his phone to check the messages. "She doesn't normally call this...." James trailed off as he scrolled up and caught sight of the first message. "I gotta go." James shoved himself to his feet quickly.

"What, other girlfriend decided to booty call him?" Brock joked dryly. Val shot him a glare before also hopping up.

"Is she okay?" Val asked softly. She may not particularly like Holly, but she was close with James and a girl frantically messaging a boy at past midnight on a Saturday wasn't exactly a calm scenario.

"Callum got drunk at Barbie's party," James told her quickly as he checked his pockets for her keys "Holly is also drunk, and they got into a fight and she just got dumped and needs a ride home." James found his keys and then stopped awkwardly to look at her. "Sorry it's just- "

"Oh no, go," Val told him quickly. "I get it." Val didn't party often and if she did it was with the same five people, but she had heard far too many horror stories of drunken girls on Saturday nights to even think of saying anything different. He had also already had quite an intense evening.

James shot her a smile and then kissed her cheek. "I'll message you later." He promised her softly before heading out the door, phone to his ear as he answered Holly's call.

"That's gonna end up being a mistake," Brock told Val sadly. Val shook her head at him before tugging at his arm as she walked past.

"Come on, you. Bedtime- I wanna hear all about your night."

Chapter Eleven

Val didn't see Jess until Monday morning. The ghost was following around Jennifer as if she was her own personal guardian angel and Val was grateful for that. Jennifer was going to need it for a little while longer.

James had given Val all of the details on Sunday, what had happened at the party and why Callum and Jennifer were now public enemy number one and two.

Some idiots that worked at the local card shop had tagged along with a friend of a friend of Barbies to the party. He had tried to make conversation with whomever he could and that included, stupidly, talking to Holly about the fact he had designed that penguin on her Valentine's Day card. There had only been one problem – on Holly's card there wasn't so much as an abstract penguin on it.

Holly had stormed over to Callum, her vodka orange spilling around her onto other people as she started to demand why he had bought two Valentine's cards and hers was the 'cheap one.' James had told Val that Holly had hoped the other card had been for his little sister.

Callum, already multiple red cups of frothy beer down, hadn't thought of that excuse and so blurted out that she was overreacting, and he had never actually done anything with Jennifer anyway. That had set off what was described as 'the fight of the year' and ended with Holly throwing the rest of her drink at Callum's face and running off to call James for a ride home.

Now poor Jennifer, whose only part in this was receiving the card in the first place, was being slandered in multiple group chats and comment sections. James had awkwardly told Val that Holly knew, deep down, that Jennifer wasn't to blame for being sent the card, but she was now second-guessing every time Callum had ever worked on a lab project.

Val had snapped that Callum had never helped Jennifer on the actual projects, only ever in class and she had hardly been living it up trying to keep her grades up with such a slouch. James had answered that he hadn't meant it like that, and the conversation went back and forth between the two of them defending their friends while still, somehow, on the same side.

It made Val dizzy just trying to think about where everyone stood now. She felt like a knight on a chessboard, only being able to move in an L shape whereas Brock and Jess were queens who could move wherever they like.

Jess was subtly getting revenge on Holly's friends when they were talking about Jennifer in a less-than-friendly fashion. Val had noticed that after Jenn and Barbie had art, Barbie had walked into the lunch hall with bright green paint all over her white shirt. Brock had burst out laughing when he caught sight of it, from his spot crouching next to Val.

"Oh, Jesus," Dylan breathed in his scratchy voice, from his place on the other side of Val. Dylan had never smoked a day in his life after his father got diagnosed with throat cancer, but his voice sounded like he smoked fifty a day. He claimed it helped him get served but considering the fact he was barely 5'5 and had peach fuzz, Val didn't believe that for a second.

"It happened in art class," Jenn mumbled as she stabbed at her undercooked pasta. "She was so busy calling me a homewrecker she didn't notice the open tub of paint by her arm."

"You're not a homewrecker," Val told her fiercely and the rest of the table agreed, although a lot less passionately. "All you did was get a card shoved into your locker. You aren't his mistress; you didn't sway him." Val carried on and she even reached over the table to squeeze her friend's arm. "This isn't your fault, it's just...high school."

"But don't worry." Jess beamed as if the table could see her as well. "I will be taking sweet, sweet vengeance for ya. There's gonna be more than green paint if the cows don't-"

The rest of Jess's friendly defensive rant was cut off as a soft silence overtook the hall. It was almost like a scene from a movie- Callum had just walked into the hall looking like he didn't have a care in the world and Holly was staring at him as if she wanted the world to hit him.

The hall wasn't completely silent but those that were talking were doing so in hushed tones and everyone seemed torn between staring or making a point to not look even remotely nearby. In Val's experience, she much preferred outright staring.

Callum joined the back of the queue for food, grabbing a juice and a snack bar as if he didn't plan to stay long. That was probably a good choice. Holly's table was getting significantly louder and a lot bolder as the seconds ticked by.

Val would have loved to say that she wasn't interested, but she was watching Callum like a hawk, same as Dylan next to her. Jennifer was twirling her pasta around her spork, staring at her plate as if it were a long lost Da Vinci sketch.

Brock had popped over to the popular table and since Val hadn't seen him move she assumed he had teleported himself or gone invisible to do so. *Very thoughtful of him either way,* Val thought as she glanced over to him. Brock had settled himself on the corner of the table next to two pretty cheerleaders and was focusing hard on Kimmy's phone. His lips were pressed together in a frown.

Val heard Dylan swear and turned to him and then over to where the small goth boy was looking. Callum had turned on his heel and was heading straight over to their table. James wasn't here, wasn't anywhere in the lunch hall as he was filming something at the local Seven-Eleven, so there was no reasonable explanation for him doing that. An unreasonable, selfish reason for him swaggering through the aisles would be to try and talk to Jennifer.

From the look in his eyes and their intense focus on the side of Jennifer's face, that seemed like exactly his plan. Jenn must have looked up, glanced to the side, or maybe she just had an extra sense like Val because the second Callum's dull brown orbs had locked on her, her hand had stilled.

Jess immediately slid in front of Jennifer, standing in the way of what Val was sure would have been a lovely and terrifying barrier if she had been alive. Jess was looking less angelic and more and more like a demon. Her jaw was set, and her lips twisted into an uncharacteristic scowl. She was set in a stance as if she was going to immediately throw a punch or was expecting a push. It made it even more heartbreaking that Callum just walked right through her.

Callum gave an awkward little shiver and Val let out an amused noise through her nose. Callum shot her an uneasy glance and fiddled with the lid on his juice. He looked at Jenn and immediately smiled.

"Hey, Jenn. We are still good to go to the library later?" Callum's voice was soft, and he had turned his body to face only her although the rest of the table were all staring at him as he had just asked her to go to Pluto for a picnic.

"I've already emailed you my half," Jennifer muttered, and she dropped her spork with a soft click. She crossed her arms and tilted her head to look up at him. Her smile was apologetic.

"Oh," Callum nodded. "Right. Yeah, I didn't check those. I just, I know I haven't been a great lab partner and you want an A for this one..."

Jennifer opened her mouth to respond and then closed it. Callum was still there and just looking at her and it made Val's skin crawl. He didn't just take the no and leave; he was waiting for her to get pressured into a response.

"Well, we were gonna go get some food after school," Val lied and loudly tapped her juice bottle against the table when Callum didn't even glance over at her. "So... answer's still no."

"Right." Callum nodded again, although he still stayed exactly where he was so Val started to think that maybe he didn't understand what a head nod meant. "Well, I'll message you," Callum told Jennifer with a smile, "and you can let me know. I'll get you my slides ASAP, Rocky, okay?"

Dylan snorted at that and quickly ducked his head when that caught Callum's attention. Callum seemed to get the hint and gave Jess a dejected wave before slowly walking backwards towards the door of the cafeteria.

"Well, that," Jess bristled from her spot at the end of the table, "was far too dramatic for a Monday." The wannabe prom queen flicked her ponytail as she looked around for Brock.

"You okay?" Val asked Jenn in a whisper, leaning over the table as Jenn shoved her pasta away from her.

"I'm fine," Jenn told her "I just didn't know what to say. I feel bad and I do want that A... it's just...I mean he's nice. He's cute."

"She needs to stop admitting that stuff in this cafeteria." Jess snapped quickly. "She's gonna make it so much worse on herself."

"Worse is already here." Brock slid across the floor and into place next to Jess. "Kimmy has decided she's having a bad day and is gonna take it out on Jenn's car. She was just doing that online stalking thing to figure out what it looks like."

"Kimmy doesn't have anything to do with this!" Jess hissed and her eyes narrowed as she looked over at the girls that were now muttering together, Barbie leaning over the table to get a better look at whatever Kimmy was drawing. If Val had to guess, then she assumed it was whatever they planned on doing to Jenn's car.

"Hey, Jenn." Val interrupted the conversation Dylan and Jenn had slipped into. "Let's skip for the rest of the day. I'm down to get some food and we can go to the mall." Val put on a grin to try and entice her friend to say yes and to get her car out of that parking lot.

"I don't know, Val," Jenn said slowly but Val pressed on.

"Are you honestly going to tell me that your gonna have complete concentration this afternoon? That any of it is going to sink into that already smart head of yours? We haven't ditched together since we were freshmen." Val rested her chin on the top of her bottle and batted her eyelashes at her. "Dylan, you'll come, right? I have my car as well; we have plenty of seats for everyone if they wanna come."

"Val makes a really good point," Dylan told her quickly. "I mean it's our last year together and it's been a hell of a day for you already."

Jenn pressed her lips together in thought and then finally relented with a soft smile. "Okay fine," she agreed, and Val and Dylan playfully cheered at her response. Jenn turned to ask the rest of the table if they wanted to come along. Val's focus turned to Holly.

Val's eyes locked eyes with Barbie instead and the girl gave a mocking little wave and smirk.

"Ohh, game on, Bitch." Jess purred.

"Jess," Brock warned softly, "be careful."

"I am being careful." Jess snapped back. "but god...she's just such a......" Jess seemed to struggle to find the exact word she wanted and settled for an animalistic grunt and clenched fists.

Brock looked over at Val as the cafeteria lights gave the slightest flicker. A few students glanced up, but most didn't pay it any mind. The lights in the school were notoriously bad due to Claire's temper tantrums and other ghosts' occasional emotional moments. Val subtly shook her head as she stretched her arms. It was nothing to worry about and frankly, if Jess was about to start world war three in the high school cafeteria, then Val would happily smash a few popular girls' heads against the table with her.

"So where are we thinking for food?" Dylan piped up as the table had decided who was and wasn't going to skip the afternoon with them.

"Jenn's choice," Val suggested immediately, "'cause let's face it, that pasta.... doesn't look great."

"It's pretty gross," Jenn agreed with a laugh. "but we should get going. Bells gonna ring soon." Val nodded her agreement and slid her jacket back on, grabbing her bag and throwing it over her shoulder within a few seconds. Jenn laughed a little at Val's urgency and slowly got all her stuff together. Dylan tried to follow Val but got himself tangled in the sleeves of his hoodie and then had to double-check he had everything in his bag.

Val had to fight the urge to tap her foot at them. They weren't aware of the ticking time bomb that was the potential car vandalism and Val couldn't exactly tell them, but she did sigh as they had to make a stop at Melissa's locker for her to grab her purse. Melissa shot her a sheepish smile.

"I just really want a doughnut. I'm low on sugar," Val muttered in explanation. She didn't talk to Melissa one on one a lot but that didn't mean she wanted her to think Val was belittling her. She was sweet, although she would often come out with a random dirty joke that left the group a mixture of disgusted and amused.

The only ones Val had a hard time stomaching were the school shooter ones, but she knew there was a lot of contexts there Melissa would have been missing. It was hard to laugh at Melissa and her white-blonde hair jokingly demanding someone brings in an AK-47 and shoots her in the head when actual victims were your best friends/roommates.

Melissa's locker was a mess, so it was no surprise when she also had trouble finding her purse. Her locker was crammed full of decorations and snacks rather than books and stationery. The inside of the door was plastered with photos of her and her girlfriend Jane, a bright green haired lifeguard at the local pool who had graduated the year before.

Val had met Jane once or twice and she was lovely, if a little condescending. The conversation had been full of 'Oh I remember back when I was a junior' and 'Oh yeah I've done that before.'

Val thought the shrine was quite sweet and she wondered if maybe she should print off some of her photos with James and put them up. Her locker was practical, full of books and a weekly calendar that she could wipe away at the end of the week.

She had some photos with Jenn, and she had very poorly edited photos of her, Brock, and Jess together that she couldn't put up for obvious reasons. She had just never thought about it before, never wanted to put part of her life up so publicly that anyone that walked past could see exactly who she adored that much.

Melissa's locker shut with a clang, and it jolted Val out of her thoughts. "Ready." Melissa chirped, and Val led the way outside to the parking lot. The February sun was giving it its best shot, but it was being blocked by large grey clouds slowly making their way across the sky.

The parking lot held a few stragglers coming back from getting lunch somewhere else or sneaking cigarettes around the side before going back in. Dylan was chatting animatedly to Jenn and Melissa about a new song he had heard from a band they all listened to. Jess and Brock had skipped ahead of the group to find Jenn's car and Brock's yell across the asphalt had Val sprinting over.

As Val got closer and her friends ran after her, she realised that she couldn't just see Brock and Jess, but at least five other people and even in the weak sunlight, Holly's multiple bangles were glistening and clicking together as she threw a smoothie all over Jenn's windshield.

"What the HELL do you think you're doing?" Val boomed at them.

"MY CAR," Jenn screamed at the same time.

Val threw her backpack down to the floor and lunged for the jacket potato that Kimmy had lifted to throw. Her hand smacked against it, and it tumbled out from Kimmy's grip and smashed against the floor.

"What's your problem?" Kimmy snarled at her and quickly moved to tuck her hair behind her ears. Val blinked twice at her. What was *her* problem? Kimmy was here throwing food and, judging by the keys that Barbie and the two boys that were with them were holding in their hands, about to scratch all sorts of things into Jenn's car.

"What the hell is wrong with you people!" Jenn reached out to gingerly touch the bright purple smoothie that was oozing all over her windshield wipers. The girl's lips were pressed together as if to stop herself from saying something harsher or to stop herself from crying. Val suspected it was the latter since she also started blinking quite quickly.

A feeling like lava shot through Val's veins at the sight and she clenched her jaw. Brock and Jess were stood mixed in with the other group, ready to grab or redirect whatever happened next. Jess was staring at the back of Kimmy's head with the intensity of a thousand Floridian suns. She was physically shaking with anger and while Brock was keeping his eye on the two boys the trio had brought with them, Val shot Jess a very slight nod.

All hell broke loose.

Chapter Twelve

That nod had been a sign for Jess to go nuts, take that ball of anger that was rolling inside of her and release it, finally, and show that just because Holly was upset about a breakup didn't mean she had any right to retaliate on Jenn.

Jess threw herself into it, just as Val hoped she would. She threw her arms around, hitting at them so they would have random cold spots and brain freezes and even went so far as to grab Kimmy's hair and yank it, so she stumbled back and fell against the asphalt.

"What's happening?!" Kimmy cried, and she threw her arms up in defence of her head even though Jess had now scooped some of the smoothies from the window and walked over to smear it all over Holly's face.

The rest of them couldn't see Jess but they could see that something had moved Kimmy, and something was moving smoothie towards Holly and Holly started walking backwards away from whatever she thought it was and even started to sob. Val couldn't help but let out a little laugh.

Maybe that made her a horrible person. The boys turned to look at her in horror, but then she saw Barbie jump at her, screaming something about a witch and she kicked out with her leg to try and keep her back, but it only stopped her for a moment. Barbie was persistent and Val let out a yelp as her long acrylic nails dug themselves into her shoulder.

"HEY." Jenn snapped out of whatever state she was in, and she started to rip away at Barbie's grip on Val. Barbie started whipping her hair around and her braids almost caught Val in the eye. Val dug her nails into Barbie's hand but as she chewed at her nails and never bothered getting them done, they were a lot less effective than the talons that Barbie had given herself.

The girl fight was over in seconds. Brock grabbed Barbie from behind and lifted her away from Val with barely a grunt. He put her down gently, on the other side of the car, but Barbie had gone shock still like a cat when picked up by the scruff of its neck.

Val turned to check on Jenn and found her best living friend was staring at her with wide eyes and a scratched lip. In the background, Val could see Dylan and Melissa's retreating backs and Val could only hope it was to go get someone to come out and stop it.

Jess had stopped her rampage, although only after she had taken Holly's keys and thrown them to the other side of the parking lot. The blonde didn't seem to care, she was just staring at Val as if she had risen from the ground with a pair of horns and a crown of bones. Brock slowly moved back to Val's side, as did Jess, although the latter walked backwards and kept her eyes on the three girls who grouped themselves together.

The two boys that were with them were now almost a whole row of cars away and from the frantic glances the girls were shooting them, they had expected the boys to be the muscle back up.

"You're gonna leave Jenn alone." Val snapped at them "No rumours. No bitchy comments. No more wrecking her stuff- and if that smoothie has done anything to her car I'm gonna make sure you.... people pay for it."

"What are you?" Barbie spat at her, and she practically dragged Kimmy to her feet and back towards where the boys were.

"Absolute freak." Kimmy sobbed.

Holly stayed silent, although she walked backwards in a slight hunch as if she was preparing to spin on her heel and run if Val so much as blinked.

"Remember that." Val snapped at them. "Next time you decide you're top of the food chain."

Once it became clear to Val that the girls weren't going to do anything else, she turned back to Jenn, who had slumped herself against the side of her car and had started taking deep breaths.

"Are you a witch?" Jenn demanded. "You're a witch right? That's what that was. That was magic or something because that wasn't normal. That wasn't right that was.... that was..."

"Intense." Val finished for her in a whisper and her body went cold as if a bucket of ice water had been thrown off her head as it fully sunk in exactly what she had done. She couldn't have stopped Jess even if she wanted to, she knew that, but she had given her a signal that this would have been okay. Her friend now thought she was a witch and maybe her other two friends had run away because they were terrified of her rather than for help.

"It's gonna be okay gorgeous," Brock told her softly, wrapping his arm around her shoulder to give it a reassuring squeeze. "This wasn't you. This was them. They did all of this, and we just retaliated, okay. They aren't hurt, not really, and no one is going to believe them, okay. I mean really- a witch. No one's gonna believe you're a witch."

"I'm not a witch." Val agreed with a nod. "Witches aren't real."

"Well, you're something." Jenn snapped. "I always knew you were a little odd, but Val you- you were stood there laughing as *something* pulled Kimmy to the ground."

"You.....you have a point there." Val laughed weakly. "But look the laugh was just a shock thing okay? That's all. It was.... I mean it's not like you saw me commanding the winds to get Barbie off of me, did you?"

"No," Jenn admitted hesitantly, after a few seconds' pause. "But then...I mean what..."

"Look it was freaky." Val agreed quickly. "But if we take this and- I mean they already blame me so- so we just- look I'm happy for them to think I'm a witch and go insane telling everybody for the next few months. I'm going to college: I don't care what they say. They are gonna leave you alone though, and we stopped them doing anything major to your car."

"I couldn't care less about my car right now. I'm more worried about if I'm going insane." Jenn struggled to get the words out.

"You're not insane," Val reassured her.

"You should tell her." Jess piped up. "You should totally tell her."

"Nope." Brock interrupted. "Do not tell her, she'll bolt."

Val wrapped her arms around Jennifer's shoulders slowly, afraid that even the slightest thing would prove Brock right and she would rush across to the parking lot. Val heard the roar of an engine and glanced up to find the three girls outside of one of the boys' Volvos, Holly screaming at the driver as Barbie and Kimmy grabbed her to stop her trying to open the door.

"What's she doing?" Jennifer was also staring at the three girls and Brock was slowly moving forward.

"Why aren't they in the car?" he asked softly. "They should.... they should be in the car right?"

Jess nodded and then suggested softly, "Maybe they aren't leaving?"

"They ran away. To a car. Surely that's them leaving?" Brock shot back but now the Volvo was driving and while it wasn't moving fast it was moving with a purpose. Jennifer realised that purpose a few seconds before Val did and she started scrambling for her keys and reaching for her driver's side door.

"No, they are not." Val shook her head, even as she could see the front of the Volvo was angled straight at them.

"Val, move!" Jenn shouted as she got into her car and stuck her keys into the ignition.

"Val," Brock called. "Val, she's right: move. Val, MOVE."

But Val didn't move. She stayed right there in front of Jennifer's car, staring at the bumper because while they may be jerks, there was absolutely no way that they would hit her. They wouldn't purposely crash into Jennifer's car and wreck it and they wouldn't smash-

"VAL, MOVE." Holly's screech across the asphalt hit home where Brock and Jennifer's hadn't and suddenly the silver-grey hunk of speeding metal seemed a lot more real, and it looked a lot closer than Val thought it should be.

The world suddenly tilted, however, as she felt someone tackle her to the ground. She felt a white-hot pain as her foot hit something hard and cold, heard the screeching of brakes and caught a glimpse of Brock's messy blonde hair before her head smacked against the floor with a thud.

Chapter Thirteen

"I know you're awake." James' voice cut through the rest of the hospital noise. "Pretending to be asleep is not gonna stop me talking at you." He gave Val's hand a gentle squeeze and Val decided to give up the ghost, as it was, and she opened up her eyes.

"Please tell me they didn't call my mum," Val told him bluntly. The hospital lights seemed brighter than usual and the beeping from machines a little louder. She had woken up in the ambulance with a frantic Brock and a crying Jess. She had been woozy and had started to tell Brock to calm down. Val's talking to people that weren't there had the paramedics checking all of her vital signs again and talking to her slowly to check she was understanding what had happened.

Val had been around enough doctors to know when they were worried. She had seen it in her father's eyes enough times to know that the paramedics were looking for brain damage. Val was lucid enough not to tell them that the fact she could see things they couldn't was a good sign. Instead, she just gave Brock a soft smile until he stopped shaking and gripped at Jess's hand until she stopped crying.

Then she got wheeled inside - *wheeled for god's sake –* and when she caught sight of James hovering around the reception area as she was being dragged past, she decided closing her eyes would be the best bet. At least, until she was put into a private room and told no visitors for a second while they got everything arranged for her. Val was starting to think that her dad keeping photos of her everywhere had some perks.

The downsides came very quickly after. Once they had made her comfortable and taken the notes from the paramedics, James had been allowed right on in while they went and got someone to do a scan on her ankle and another check-up.

"You got hit by a car in the school parking lot. They had to call your mum and I heard a nurse calling for your dad as well." James told her with an awkward, almost apologetic smile.

Val groaned dramatically and threw her head softly back against her fluffed pillows. "God, he's going to go mental."

"Oh, don't you worry, princess." A new voice echoed into the room as a lanky Asian man in his early twenties stepped into the room and closed the door behind him. He shot Val a cheeky, full-face grin and she raised her eyebrow at him.

"Come to laugh at me, Milo?" Val turned her head to look at him.

"Your dad's finishing up surgery and I heard why they were calling. Figured I'd head over to do your check-up for you." Milo told her, and he walked over to throw himself into the other available chair.

"So." Milo smiled at her. "Paramedics say you were seeing people that weren't there on the way in. You still see me?"

Milo's head was down, reading through some notes but James shot her an uneasy look.

"No," Val answered confidently. It was true- Jess had run off to find her father and give him an update on his way over. If he was in surgery, then she was probably just waiting for him to finish up. Brock was the one she was worried about. She assumed he would be at her side constantly, threatening the boys in the Volvo with all sorts of torture and slang that Val would have to google later. But he had left her as soon as she was put into this room.

Milo looked up as if he didn't believe her but when Val scowled at him, he simply nodded. "So, you got into a car accident in the school parking lot? How very freshman of you." Milo teased.

"It's not a car accident if I'm just stood there. Besides, the car didn't really hit me." Val told him, and she adjusted her blanket.

"You weren't even in a car." Milo paused, frowning as he looked through his notes. "Oh my god, your mom is going to kill them."

"Yep," Val agreed with a hard 'p' and a head nod. "Which is why dads are supposed to be the primary contact."

"Your dad was in surgery, and they had to call an ambulance. They had to call somebody, legally." Milo told her absentmindedly as he added something to the notes. Val watched him scratch away with his biro and then sighed. This was a big mess.

"Wait- is Jenn okay?" Val asked and looked over at James. James nodded and gave her hand yet another squeeze.

"Jenn's fine. Tim and Roger chickened out at the last minute when they saw you weren't moving, and they were gonna hit more than the front of Jenn's car. Your ankle is the only thing they hit just as you leapt out of the way. Kimmy got the whole thing on camera." James explained softly. "The girls feel just terrible, Val-"

Val cut him off with a harsh laugh and felt the lava-like feeling spreading over her body again. "They vandalised Jenn's car. They threw food over it; they were going to key it and if we hadn't stopped them, they may have just decided to completely wreck it anyway. All because *your friend* sent her a Valentine's Day card."

"Jesus Christ, what is your high school?" Milo muttered but both James and Val heard him and shot him a scowl. "I'm just saying," Milo said in his defence, "that that is incredibly extreme."

Val gestured to Milo with a triumphant look at James who frowned but didn't have a counterargument. "I just know that Holly feels horrible about it. She's the one that called me. I think she's going to pop by after she finishes talking to the cops if you're up for it."

"Like a shot to the head," Val said icily. James recoiled slightly at that, and Milo gave an awkward shuffle. "Her feeling bad as her friends already speeding head-on to hit us doesn't make her my friend all of a sudden. She can be yours, but the day I willingly spent time with her is the day all seven circles of hell freeze over."

James slowly slid his hand out from under Val's and stared at her for a moment. The air felt heavy, and the room was deadly silent except for the sound of Milo's papers rubbing together as he re-read the same page.

"You're right," James said softly "I know you're right. It's just...It's insane to me that she went that far."

Val's anger died down a little then, the lava feeling in her veins cooling to that of a sauna as she saw how sad that realisation made James. "It's not like she was driving," Val said slowly.

"Your ankle only looks badly sprained." Milo chimed in as he finished with her notes and then without warning lifted the blanket at her feet and started to gently probe at it with his fingers.

Val hissed and pulled her leg back "You can tell that just by looking? You don't look like an X-ray machine."

"Your dad is a good teacher."

"My dad's a surgeon- he doesn't check out people hurt ankles."

"It's a basic medical skill." Milo pulled the blanket down. "I'll get you an ice pack and some pain meds, but you're not gonna need an X-ray unless you insist on one."

Val shook her head at that. She knew that it was important to make sure her foot was okay, she was going to need it, but if Milo was sure it was a sprain, and the pain didn't feel bad enough to be a break, then she was happy to accept that.

"What about my concussion?" Val asked him bluntly. The paramedics had confirmed she had one, right after checking her head for a break and blood. While her head was hurting, and everything was slightly out of focus, she was told that after a few days she would be 'completely fine again.'

"Your dad knows all the things to do with that. Rest up for a few days, no driving, and try not to watch TV. You can still read through, so you're all good there." Milo told her absentmindedly as he checked his watch. Val nodded at him.

"Awesome," Val said sarcastically.

"At least you won't have to go to school," James told her, starting to trace his fingers over her arm. "That's a bonus."

"Because when I do I'll just die of the embarrassment of it?" Val quipped.

"You're gonna be embarrassed when someone else tried to hit you with a car?" Milo scoffed.

"I'm just that hated at school."

"Oh, you're gonna love college though," Milo said encouragingly. "Everyone's a bit weird at college. Especially that nice big ivy league you applying to."

"You talk to my dad way too much," Val told him, and she felt the familiar pinprick of heat in her cheeks.

"I'm one of his interns. Constantly by his side is how I learn," Milo responded smoothly before placing his notes on the side table. "Once your mum is here, you'll be free to go."

As if the words had summoned her, Charlie Ellis appeared at the doorway looking like she was ready to fight the devil himself. She walked with purpose, and she was wearing a black leather jacket and jeans. She looked like she had walked straight out of a cop show. As soon as her eyes caught on her daughter in a hospital bed, her face softened. Val opened her mouth to explain but her mother had pulled her into a hug.

"You are never going back to that school," she told her bluntly. "I knew we should have looked into home-schooling or online classes. That place has been trouble from the get-go and now, now you're being run down by some utter- "

"Mom, I am not dropping out of school," Val interrupted her quickly, "and I wasn't run down, it hit my ankle- "

"After they vandalised your friend's car!" Charlie pulled back and held her daughter's head gently in her hands. "We are going to sort this out before you step a single inch onto that school's property. I'm gonna get those kids' names, ALL of them, and when I am done- "

"Honey," Daniel Ellis warned from the hallway, straight out of surgery and in fresh scrubs. "Let her breathe a little. She's been under a lot of stress today."

"Very stressed," Val agreed with vigorous head nods that she instantly regretted as it made her head hurt. Charlie raised her delicate eyebrows at her daughter but relented.

"Well, I'll leave you guys alone. Feel better Val." Milo shot her a wink as he left the room. Charlie quickly took the seat that he had vacated and started running her thumbs up and down the back of Val's hand. Between her and James, Val felt like a drawing pad. She gently pulled arms out of their reach, and she propped herself up into a seated position.

Val turned her attention to her dad. "Have you seen Brock?"

Daniel shook his head. "Jess was waiting in the surgery for me but then she disappeared. I thought she came here."

Val's frown mirrored her father's. "No. They came in the ambulance with me, but they vanished when I got here. Brock was the one that pushed me out of the way."

"Dear god I love that boy." Charlie breathed and looked around the room as if saying that would summon the boy she couldn't see to the room.

"You didn't move out the way?" James asked softly and Val was too ashamed to look at him. She looked down at her hands and shook her head.

"It's an intense situation. You froze, that's okay." Daniel told his daughter as he moved towards her and sat on the end of her bed. "You banged your head and sprained your ankle. I don't care how you got out of the way as long as you did."

"It just feels so stupid. I just stood there and watched it, thinking how they just wouldn't hit me." Val looked up at her mother from under her lashes. "I just thought I was smarter than that."

"You're ridiculously smart," Charlie told her daughter immediately "and so beautiful. You just think the best of people and that is something I need you to keep, okay? Me and your dad are far too cynical."

"I don't even like birthday parties anymore." Daniel agreed with a nod. "People at them just suck."

Val laughed and James joined in. The teenage couple looked at each other and this time Val reached over to grab his hand. James' smile turned soft as they both started to play with the others fingers.

"Thank you." Daniel turned to look at James. "For getting here so fast and sitting with her. I fear I would have walked into a dead intern on the floor if she were left alone with Milo."

"I like Milo!" Val argued, "I just prefer him when he's not speaking."

The Ellis family all laughed at that, and Daniel leaned over to kiss his daughter's forehead. "I'm glad that concussion hasn't taken away your sense of humour."

Chapter Fourteen

After he had checked in with his family, Daniel still had some paperwork to finish, and he wanted to check on some of his younger patients' recoveries. Charlie insisted on going out and getting 'the kids' some food as she insisted that Val did get an X-ray done just to be safe, and a CT scan.

Val managed to convince the doctor that the CT scan was overkill and there was no need to clog up the queue for something as basic as a concussion. The X-ray she didn't get out of so easily, but James stayed with her as much as possible while her mum went to grab them some 'actual food' from a take-out nearby. Charlie may love visiting her husband at work, but she avoided hospital food like the plague.

Brock and Jess crashed into Val's private room, Jess once again near tears and Brock looking as angry as Val had ever seen him. He slammed the door shut and he was panting. Val realised as he turned his head to look at her that it wasn't anger in his eyes. It was fear.

"Brock, what's going on?" Val asked softly, ignoring that James had jumped at the door slam.

"H-He's here." Jess sobbed wildly. "Val, he's here." Jess had curled herself up into a ball against the wall beside the door.

"Who's here, Jess?" Val asked softly and started to untangle herself from the blankets and she crouched down in front of the ghost girl. Her ankle buckled beneath her, but she caught herself just in time. "Jess it's okay, it's okay." Val ran her hands up and down the girl's arms. She heard James's chair squeak against the floor as he got up to follow her.

"Logan Pierce." Brock ground out through a clenched jaw as he looked around the hall through the small window in the door. Val snapped her head up to look at Brock and then back down at Jess and shook her head in disbelief.

"Logan Pierce isn't a ghost," Val reminded them bluntly. "Remember? You and Claire and everyone looked for him and he'd just not stuck around."

"Well, we were wrong." Brock snapped at the same time as James asked Val, "What's going on?"

"He was with your dad earlier. He was watching his surgery and I just- I just froze and I needed to find Brock and-" Jess hid her face in her hands and start hyperventilating. Val wrapped her arm around her and started to repeat as a chant, "You're safe. He can't hurt you."

"Val. What. Is. Going. On," James asked her slowly, looking up as there were flickering lights outside and inside the room. Val took a deep breath to answer him but then stopped as she saw that the breath she had released, she could physically see in the air. The temperature had dropped so quickly that she hadn't even started to properly feel it yet.

"Logan's ghost is here." Val whispered. "He was- "

"He was the shooter." James quickly moved to the door, right through Brock. He shuddered at that, and Brock snapped an insult at him. Val shot him a confused look at that, she was sure she had never told him, but then the lights turned completely off, and Jess let out a strangled scream in the three seconds before they turned back on.

"Jesus." Brock stumbled back and when Val looked up, she saw a face staring into the room.

Logan Pierce didn't look like a stereotypical school shooter. He had no dark clothes or guyliner on. There were no heavy metal logos on his shirt. He wasn't small and weedy.

He was completely average.

His hair was brown and shaggy, he was half a head shorter than Brock and his only memorable feature was a small mole in the centre of his chin. He wasn't ugly exactly, but the way his face was contorted in rage as he stared at Brock was so terrifying, Val recoiled.

"James, get away from the door," Val begged softly, and James furrowed his brows at her before doing as she asked.

"Why is he here? At the hospital?" James kept his eyes on the door even though they all knew that he couldn't tell if anything was going on. "I mean, I know he died here but it's been decades. Why would he care about you guys right now?"

Val went to answer and then stopped and turned to look at Jess, whose head was still hidden away in her arms as if she was refusing to be a part of this situation.

"He saw Jess," Brock answered, and his voice went hoarse. "He tried to speak to her, but she came and found me instead. He found her again. He was trying to apologise and Jess just...She snapped. She screamed at him for what he did, and he screamed back and it just...." Brock trailed off and Val looked between Jess and Logan.

Logan tilted his head to look down at Val and gave her a mocking little wave.

"Hey!" Brock boomed and walked over to slam his hand against the window. Brock was practically vibrating with rage and when Logan simply smiled at him, Brock's response was less of a smile and more a baring of teeth.

James looked around the room as if he was waiting for something to happen. Something to be thrown or smashed to let him know the ghosts were inside. Val was simply staring at Brock with wide eyes.

"Brock, what does he want this time?" Val's voice was shaky and frightened like a child without a night light. "Why didn't he just leave?"

"It's my fault," Jess whispered back. "I was bragging. Bragging that he had been left all alone and that we...weren't."

Val went completely still then, and she took a few deep breaths, so she didn't join Jess in her panic. Brock didn't have to say anything, Jess didn't have to continue. Jess had angered her murderer and told him that her afterlife was going better than his. This was a messed-up teenager who had killed his classmates because he felt so alone. What was he going to do to the girl who had made his victim's afterlives bearable?

"He's going to kill me," Val breathed. She thought saying it out loud would make her calm down, help her rationalise the fact that these next few moments would be her last— and potentially James. Val pulled herself to her feet with a painful grimace.

James had heard her, that was apparent by how quickly he moved in front of her and cupped her head in his hands. "You are not about to die."

Val rested her hands over his and gave him a small smile. She wanted to apologise for scaring him, for being the reason that he was here right now and there was a ghost of a murderer outside just waiting to come in. But that would just hurt him more, scare him when hopefully she could find a way for him to get out of this okay.

"I love you," Val whispered instead. "and if anything does start happening, I want you to run, okay. Jess will just drag you out if you don't." Val lied before forcing her lips up into a soft smile. Val could see him go to argue, so she continued quickly,, "Find my dad. Someone who can see."

James' jaw was clenched, and Val moved her hands, so they were placed on his cheeks instead. She started gently rubbing her thumbs on his cheekbones. "Promise me," Val begged softly. "Please."

James took a deep breath through his nose and then slowly nodded his head. That was enough for Val. She leant forward to kiss him. James kissed her back fiercely and they stayed like that for a moment. Val was glad that her last few moments were something so simple, so loving. She was almost at peace. She thought that was probably helped along by the fact that she knew she would come back. She would still have her friends and her father and to a certain aspect her mother. James would know she was still around. She wasn't going into this blindly.

"I got this." Brock took three long strides towards the door and came to a stop next to the three of them. Val looked up at him confused, James following her gaze. Jess shot to her feet then and shook her head at him.

"Brock..." Jess trailed off. "Brock, we can wait him out."

"I'm not risking it," Brock said bluntly, and he turned to look at Logan, who looked almost bored as he watched them. Brock looked down at Val, who was trying to move around James. She put a little too much weight on her ankle and she winced.

"Brock, it's okay," Val told him, although the sight of him there, standing tall and rolling his shoulders to get ready to go out there and face the teenager that had left him gasping for air on a high school floor...that was what finally brought her to tears.

"It's not. None of this is okay but this is happening and the day I let you die is the day I deserve to be shot up." Brock told her. They locked eyes and the tears streamed down Val's face. Brock gave her a sad half-smile.

"You can't." Val insisted with a head shake. "You're my best friend. You can't die. You can't leave me. It's fine, Brock, it's okay, really, I'll just- I'll just end up with you guys forever and that's okay, I'm okay with that so just don't just please, please don't."

Val's begging was paired with shoulder-shaking sobs. The only thing keeping Logan out of the room right now was Jess and Brock. Their combined powers that Val had never given a name to or perhaps just the fact that Logan liked to toy with them- that's what had let Val have her final kiss.

"I can't let that happen to you." Brock turned his head to lock eyes with Logan. "I love you, Val." With that admission, Brock stepped right through the doorway to a waiting Logan.

Val lunged for the door, screaming "Brock" as she tried to yank it open. Her fingertips just touched the handle before she felt someone yank her back. She started to elbow at them and struggled to get to the door. If she could just get there, if she could just get outside then it would be fine, and Brock would be okay and-

"Val please." Jess begged in her ear. "Please. It's done, it's done now. I'm not letting you out of that door."

Val felt another pair of arms wrap around her. In compar-
ison to Jess's, they felt like fire and Val realised that James
had joined in. She stopped her scrambling for the door then
and just silently sobbed in both their arms. She would never
get past both of them, not with her ankle.

Chapter Fifteen

Brock took a deep breath once he was in the hall. Logan was just as scrawny as he remembered. There was no gun this time, nothing to tip the scales in his direction. They were just both undead teens that could move things with their minds and opposing goals.

"You're not getting in that room," Brock told Logan bluntly as he took a stance in front of the door and flexed his fingers out of their fists.

"Funny." Logan shot back in a voice that suggested it was anything but. "You said that last time."

"It's different this time." Brock shifted his shoulders. "No gun for a start."

"And your little psychic girlfriend's inside making out with her actual boyfriend. Are you more worried about her not coming back like we did or the fact he might come back with her?" Logan tilted his head with a smirk. That smirk turned into a smile as he saw Brock's jaw snap shut.

"I mean if you ask real nicely," Logan taunted, "I could not kill him. That way, little Val has to be stuck just like you. She won't be so happy then, huh? Having to watch her boyfriend forget about her. Her father being the only one able to see her. Daniel is such a lovely doctor: it's a shame to do it to him. But then, according to Jess-"

"Didn't you call her collateral damage last time?" Brock interrupted. "It was very satisfying watching you die. Here, on one of those comfy beds, giving your little, I'm sorry speech."

Logan's face turned even sourer, but Brock carried on. The angrier that he made Logan the easier it would be to win.

"I got to bleed out on a cold floor that smelt like too much bleach. You tried to shoot yourself and Claire is the one that ruined that for you. Isn't that just so poetic? Your main target kicked out her leg in a *death spasm* and your gun just doesn't hit the right spot. I hope even through all that morphine there was a deep agonising pain." Brock was tempted to start circling Logan like a lion does his prey, but he didn't want to give up his spot in front of the door.

"Typical of all of you, ya know that. You all die, and you still end up having a lovely time in high school." Logan snapped, and he took a step forward. "I mean, god, it would almost be pathetic. You all just hang around there all the time like you are permanently stuck in senior year."

"Well, someone cut ours pretty short," Brock reminded him. "Ya know, some psycho brought in his dad's handgun and started blasting away."

"Don't call me psycho." Logan snarled. "You people made my life hell for three and a half years."

"Oh, so you decide to just try and send us all to actual hell?"

"Well, isn't that something? You think you belong in hell too!" Logan let out a laugh then. "Has it taken you two decades to realise you were a massive tool?"

"Have you realised after spending two decades in a hospital watching people die that you had no god damn right to do what you did?" Brock's blood started to boil- or at least, it felt like it did.

Earlier when he had seen Jess, Logan's face had resembled something similar to remorse. He had even tried to apologise to her, but it had only taken one rejection to have Logan spiralling back into a murderous mood.

"I like to think of what I did as a public service. You ruined my life- "

"I'll think you'll find the mass murder did that."

"STOP INTERRUPTING ME," Logan screamed at him and the lights in the hall once again flickered. Brock saw from the corner of his eye that the nurses and hospital visitors looked around uneasily but just shrugged it off. Val had once mused that it was easier to blame poor funding and cheap lightbulbs than to believe that ghosts exist. He was going to miss her way of explaining the supernatural away.

Logan was panting now, like a rabid dog, and Brock shifted forward slightly. He trusted Jess to keep the barrier up until this was over. She had been scared earlier but she was a good person, and a good person wouldn't let Val die. Jess cared about her too much to watch it happen.

"You and your friends were vermin. Pretty vermin are still vermin and Claire deserved it. You deserved it. Every single one of you deserved it. Even Jess- she let it all slide, was still friends with you all after what you people did to everyone." Logan was gesturing around wildly, swinging his arms into people without a care.

"What has Val done, exactly?" Brock demanded. "Except be kind to a couple of desperate ghosts who were stuck without their families for twenty years?"

"Don't start talking to me about family." Logan reached forward to poke at Brock's chest. "Mine moved away. They didn't even defend me, not even in private. My mum just cried herself into a wine problem about how she should have known."

"Well...she should have," Brock whispered, and he knew that was the final straw. He had heard enough on the radio, theorised with his friends about it over the last two decades to know that if there was one thing that Logan had, it was a mommy complex.

Logan lunged for him, and Brock managed to twist them, so they fell on their sides on the floor. Brock had been in a few fights before, back when he was alive, and he normally would have his full body weight as an advantage but now...now they were just two angry ghosts.

The lights were flickering faster now in the hall and a toddler that was playing on the floor started to cry as the ghosts rolled over him. But Brock wasn't focussing on that as he ended up on top of his opponent. With every punch and knee and grab, Brock thought of Val.

Val laughing so hard she snorts, even when they are watching a stupid sitcom way before her years. The loops Val made in her capital L's. The awkward little hop around the floor she always did when she stubbed her toe. How she danced mostly with her hands, and she was horrible with her hips.

Brock hit him harder and harder with every thought and as he heard Val sobbing for him in her room, Brock wrapped his hands around Logan's neck. The mass murderer stopped trying to kick Brock off and focused on getting his hands off of his throat.

"I want you to know," Brock ground out, "that I could have let it go. I could have forgiven you. All you had to do..." Brock gave his throat a quick squeeze, "was leave her out of it."

Logan tried to choke out an answer, but Brock just grabbed his hair and slammed his head down against the cold tiles. "No," Brock told him softly. "You don't get to speak. You don't get any dramatic final words this time. You just get to look up at me. You didn't wanna look at me last time- but you're sure as hell gonna look at me now."

Chapter Sixteen

Val was limp in James's arms, but she was staring at the window in the wall as if it was a portal to another world. She wanted Brock to step into that little rectangle of light and shoot her a grin. His hair would be as messy as ever and she would wrap him in a hug so tight that if he had lungs she would be afraid of suffocating him.

"He'll be fine." Jess tried to reassure her although when she reached out to gently touch Val's arm, she had flinched away as if her finger were tiny daggers. "I mean...he's already dead."

"Exactly." Val snarled. "So, who knows what could happen to him. Last time you and Claire had a fight you both couldn't be.... you for days. What if Brock is stuck like that forever?"

The idea of Brock losing his ghost body, stuck forever unable to speak to anyone or move anything, just watching everything float by had Val's heart beating louder and louder in her chest. She was sure James could hear it from the worried staring and her lungs suddenly felt too small, and her breathing turned into gasps.

"Brock will win this time," Jess reassured her, and she roughly put Val's head onto James' chest. "Now calm down. Listen to his heartbeat and just wait. Your dad's gonna be coming back and Brock is going to be fine."

Jess's babble was fierce and hearing her be so confident in their friend gave Val something else to focus on. Jess was right. Brock would be fine, and he would win this time. He had spent years after his death antagonising himself for the fact he failed. This was his redemption and Val had read enough books, watched enough shows to know that the hero gets his redemption.

The prince gets the girl. The dog gets his owner back. Brock Walker gets to walk in through that door.

Chapter Seventeen

James wrapped his arm around Val's shoulder and gently ran his hands over the back of her head. He tried to stay calm by taking deep breaths and not tapping his foot although he felt like he had just been electrocuted. He was full of energy and worry and the ball of that in his stomach felt as heavy as lead.

Val had been ready to die. He couldn't hear two-thirds of the conversation, but he knew that Brock and Jess wouldn't let that happen. Val's screams confirmed he was right- she had lunged for the door exclaiming Brock's name like it was her own personal lord's prayer and James had to hold her back. A small part of his brain wondered if she would ever forgive him for that.

Ever since he had got that call from Holly about Val and the car, James had known something wasn't right. Holly had started babbling about how Tim and Roger thought that Val was a demon and they tried to hit her with the car and now there was an ambulance at the school but by that point, James was already rushing back to his car. The blue slushie prop he had gone to the seven eleven for would be long since melted, what had remained in the cup after he had spilt it all over his centre console in his rush.

He wanted to tell Val that this would be okay. That the friends of hers that he couldn't see would be fine and that he would never, even to himself, say anything bad about

Brock if he would just come back in and take that look off of her face.

James pressed a gentle kiss to the top of her head, and she nuzzled into him. Her eyes were red, and her face was covered in both old and new tears. She was squinting in the direction of the window and James silently hoped that no one out there was epileptic. The yellow-tinted lights had practically become strobe lights while they waited safely in here.

He vaguely wondered what would happen at the end. Would the door burst open? Would Val let him know or would she be so thoroughly destroyed by the result that she would never tell him?

That thought had him strengthening his hold on her. She had shown him- or rather, told him- a whole other part of the world and even if he physically couldn't see it, he also couldn't let it go. He had watched Valkyrie Ellis ever since her moving van had driven past his street. She had been a cool breeze in an otherwise stagnant town. It made complete sense to James that she was special enough to see things others couldn't.

It didn't make sense to him that she was so willing to die or that she had made James promise to just leave her behind. James didn't know how to bring that up or even if he should. He loved her and he wouldn't leave her no matter what, invisible enemy or a mortal one.

"Val, I..." James trailed off. Val tilted her head up to face him, but her eyes remained fixed on that entrance. James breathed out through his nose and placed a gentle kiss on her temple. Somehow, she had wiped her tears that far up her face and his lips came away salty.

James was caught in a whirlwind of thoughts about what to say to her that he almost missed it when the lights stopped flickering. There was a shift in the room, however and he felt an acute coldness on his arm.

"Brock?" James guessed lowly.

"Try again, sport." Brock boomed as he stepped into the room.

It took James a few seconds to process everything. The first thing was that Val was out of his arms quicker than he had ever seen anything move. His girlfriend wrapped her arms around a tall, muscular blonde boy with tousled hair. The second thing he processed was that the blonde was almost glowing with pure white light. The third thing, and the thing that he should have realised first, was that he could see Brock Walker.

He had seen pictures. He had looked into the victims and the shooting after Val told him. But no amount of research could have prepared him for the real thing. He was taller than he looked in pictures and the grin he shot Val as he spun her around in a circle could never have been captured in a photo.

There was no blood on him, and James was almost proud of the fact he noticed that before Val. Val had told him that ghosts kept their wounds but here Brock Walker was, faintly glowing and completely fine.

"I knew you'd be okay." Val had her hands on Brock's shoulders and her smile took up her entire face. She gave him a gentle shake and then laughed once before hugging him to her again.

James had been a little sceptical about Val spending every minute of her day with Brock but had been reassured multiple times that there was nothing more than platonic between them. James supposed it would have been easy to lie to him about it. The look in Brock's eyes told James all he ever needed to know about exactly what would have happened if Brock had been a living, breathing teen.

Val looked randomly to the side and then back at Brock. She gingerly reached out to lay her hand on the middle of his torso. "Jess is right." Val whispered. "you're not hurt anymore."

"I just came to say goodbye." Brock reached out and gently held Val's elbows. "I only have a few minutes." Brock's voice was soft, reassuring even though Val's face showed that she didn't buy it. James didn't either.

"What do you mean, 'goodbye,' you're coming home with me," Val told him bluntly, her voice on the verge of panic.

"I'm moving on Val." Brock gently started to rub at her arms and James suddenly felt completely out of place rather than one foot in the door. This moment was more private than anything he had ever seen, and it was hard to look at.

"My unfinished business was kicking Logan's ass. I just didn't want you to think something bad was happening." Brock continued and then pulled Val into a bear hug.

"I don't want you to go." Val's voice cracked as she hid her face in his neck. "I told you. You aren't allowed to leave me."

"I'm always going to be with you. I'll be an actual guardian angel for you now," Brock joked weakly. "Just...more silent."

"My favourite part is your stupid voice." Val's voice was muffled.

"That's because you never made out with me. Wanna give it a shot before I head off to heaven?" Brock then let out a laugh as Val pinched at his side. Brock's eyes then latched onto James.

"Yeah, Jess, I know," Brock whispered although he kept his gaze on James. James felt like he was now under a microscope, and he awkwardly shuffled into a standing position and squared his shoulders.

"It's nice to finally meet you." James choked out and Val looked between the two boys with a small frown.

"You can see him?" Val asked and James nodded his response.

"Everyone can see me right now," Brock informed her softly, "and in a couple of seconds no one is ever gonna see my gorgeous face again."

Val let out a choked sound at that and James took a step to go to her, but Brock simply wrapped her in another hug.

"It's okay, gorgeous, it's okay." Brock insisted "It's my time. I should have moved on years ago."

"You're not scared?" Val looked up at Brock with a look of absolute wonder. Brock shook his head at her and squeezed her. The two then looked over at something that James assumed was Jess and he had an idea. It would either end terribly or Val would adore him for it. As they were distracted, James slowly slipped his phone from his pocket.

Val looked back over at him just in time for a few shots. She opened her mouth to say something but turned back to Brock and the space and simply smiled instead.

"Thank you." Brock interrupted James and then slowly walked over to James and held out his hand. James looked at it for a second and then put his phone away so that he could shake it.

Brocks handshake was firm, but his hands were surprisingly soft, and James looked down at them, puzzled. Brock let out a breathy laugh and took his hand back. "I like you by the way. As much as I reasonably could." Brock put his hands into the pockets of his jeans.

James' face twitched into an amused smile. "Because we both love her?"

"Because you're a good person. She deserves that." Brock said, and James suddenly felt almost guilty for the assumption. That was until Val made her way over and Brock turned his head to look at her.

Val settled herself in-between the two boys and then both her and Brock laughed. James was clearly missing a large part of the goodbyes and then what was a group hug. Brock pulled back from the hug looking somehow even brighter than before.

Val noticed as well because her smile lost its glow. "You're leaving," she told Brock and the teenager nodded his head.

"You sure you don't want to give me that goodbye kiss? James can't get mad at you for a goodbye kiss." Brock teased her and while Val's lip twitched slightly, the smile was still almost completely gone.

"I'm never gonna see you again, am I?" Val reached desperately for Brock's hand, but it went almost completely through him. He was now so bright James was squinting slightly.

"Not for many, many decades," Brock told her. The two stared at each other for a moment as Brock faded from view. Just before he was completely encompassed by the glowing white light, Brock winked at Val.

Val's response was a magnificent grin- until all of the light went from the room with a flash. Then she fell to her knees crying and James dove to the floor to catch her, as he always would.

Chapter Eighteen

Daniel Ellis had seen many things in this life. He had met many ghosts and argued with most of them, but he had never mourned one as much as he did Brock Walker. Val had been quiet, even when he had found her curled up on top of the hospital bed with James. He had heard about the flickering lights from passing nurses. He had assumed that Jess or Brock had gotten emotional about someone trying to hit Val with a car. It had never occurred to him that it would be something else.

Val's concussion was the perfect excuse to keep her out of school for the rest of the week, not that he could have forced her to go even if he wanted to. She had become a shell of herself, only eating when Charlotte brought her something or reminded her and staring numbly at a book since her mother had also gently reminded her that she shouldn't be staring at a screen with her injury.

Jess had been solemn for a day or two before making an effort to go back to her normal self. She had softly explained to Daniel, the morning of the change as Daniel was buttering some toast for his daughter, that Brock would have wanted her to look after Val. Daniel had to blink away the tears pooling in his eyes before he had gone to joined his daughter on the sofa.

James had forwarded the photos he had taken in the hospital room of Brock and Val. Val had cried over them and refused to talk to anyone about it. Daniel and Charlie had a rare, intense argument when he found out that she had quietly asked James for copies as well. The plan was to print them for Val for her room as a surprise to help the grieving. Daniel had hidden the photos away for the moment.

Val was currently curled up on the couch with Oz and a mountain of blankets. As he walked back into the house, Val looked up at him with an ashamed smile. "How did she take it?" Val asked as she propped herself up into a sitting position. Oz stirred from his position as the little spoon but stayed where he was.

"Not well," Daniel admitted as he sat himself down on the armrest of the sofa next to his daughter's head. He leant down and gently ran his hand up and down her arm. "But I think she's happy that her son is in a better place. She said she wanted to come by and see how you're doing when you're feeling well enough."

Daniel thought that was either a horrible idea or the best one to ever have been thought up. Mrs Walker had been distraught the second she saw him on her doorstep. She had known, deep down, that Brock was never coming home for the second time.

Val sunk in on herself at that question and she took a deep breath as she figured out what to say. Daniel, knowing his daughter as well as he did, knew that it was going to be an excuse on why that was a bad idea. Daniel knew that Val wanted to be alone but as he watched her ignore her phone as it lit up on the table, he also knew that if he didn't do something then this was going to be a hole she may not climb out of.

"I think it would be good," Daniel told her quickly, "to have the people that loved Brock all talking about him."

"His funeral was twenty years ago," Val told her father bitterly. "That would have been all the people that loved him. She's already been through it once. She doesn't need to do it again."

"Valkyrie, that's not your decision to make," Daniel told his daughter softly but firmly. "You're upset. I am too. But she's Brock's mother and he's gone and- "

"And her pain is worse?" Val snapped at her father, and she recoiled from him, disrupting Oz as she moved. "I know Jess told you everything. I know you know what he said and why he did it."

Daniel had been praying he didn't have to have this part of the conversation. He knew he was the father of a teenage girl but there was no chapter in any of the parenting books about what to say to your daughter after her ghost best friend tells her he loves her and fights his murderer to keep her safe.

"It's not your fault. It was Brock's decision. He would make it over and over again and we all know that. You were going to make it for him, weren't you? You were gonna sit in that room and let someone murder you, Valkyrie." Daniel's voice turned hard then. "You were going to leave us on purpose."

"You didn't see Jess's face. You didn't hear her crying." Val started to speak over her dad "And I knew that I would never really leave you- "

"But you would never grow up either!" Daniel yelled and after he raised his voice, the two stared at each other. Val's breathing was erratic as if she was trying to stop crying again and that broke Daniel's heart in two.

"All I've ever wanted is you safe and happy." Daniel slid himself down onto the sofa next to her. Oz climbed down from the sofa complete with a huff. Daniel didn't even spare the dog a glance as he pulled his daughter into his chest and hugged her. "And it breaks my heart to think of you in that room accepting the fact you weren't going to be anymore."

There was a silence then and Daniel just listened to his daughter steady her breathing.

"I'm sorry dad." Val whispered, "I'm so sorry."

"It's okay sweetie," Daniel responded immediately. "I'm sorry I yelled, I just...I don't want to lose you. Even if it's just the living you. I want you to go to college, adopt some animals, and move into a tiny apartment to try and figure out how to cook the right amount of pasta. I want to walk you down the aisle and panic buy you furniture when you buy a house. I can't do any of that if you decide your life isn't worth anything because you know you can just stick around."

"I know my life is worth something," Val mumbled. "I just think that Brock's was worth more."

Daniel had to try and swallow the lump that was suddenly stuck in his throat. "No one is ever worth more than you," Daniel promised her in a whisper.

Chapter Nineteen

Those eight words echoed around Val's head for the following two days. Her head was feeling better and so was her ankle, but she enjoyed the excuse to stay in bed and her mother was enjoying pampering her.

Jess had disappeared the day before, after Val had snapped at her to stop being so happy all the time. Val assumed she was spending that time with Claire although she could have sworn that she heard her father whispering and Jess answering just as quietly in other rooms.

Claire had arrived just after with dramatic stories and anecdotes about Brock. How brave and hot he was, how his being a secret nerd was so endearing and it made Val want to follow up on her promise to exorcise her. Her father had taken the hit and dealt with Claire from then on and whatever excuse he had used, she hadn't been around since.

"You sure you're gonna be okay?" Charlie called as she came in from the kitchen with yet another smoothie for her daughter. She had decided that if her daughter wasn't going to eat her vitamins, then she could drink them. "I can call in sick to work and be here with you."

"And let the citizens of Drayton go without their favourite blonde detective?" Val teased her mother. "I wouldn't dream of it."

"Pretty sure that Susan is their favourite blonde detective."

"Well, that's because she never wears underwear. Pervy teenage boys are a constant no matter the town," Val quipped back as she took the smoothie from her. "But seriously I'll be fine. It's just Mrs Walker. This talk is going to be good for me."

Val's words were an echo of her father's from breakfast when he caught Val constantly checking the time on her phone. It would be a nice sort of closure for her, was the other part of the argument and while Val would love to agree, she remembered the look on Mrs Walker's face that night she had figured it out. She had spent the last two nights imagining how much worse her face would be today.

Charlie settled herself in the armchair in the corner of the room as she watched Val sip at the bright purple concoction. Val knew there was another question coming. Her mother was adoring but she usually settled for just handing over the drink and trusting Val would drink it.

"Have you spoken to James today?" Charlie started rubbing her hands together and Val took a long noisy sip.

Val had responded to her boyfriend's messages, but they were never overly enthusiastic. He was giving her space and letting her mourn, although Val wasn't stupid enough to think that it wouldn't affect their relationship. Holly's get well soon/I'm sorry message had been left on read ever since Val got home from the hospital. She was letting her parents deal with the parking lot incident. It felt far too separate from everything to care about it fully.

"I'm gonna message him in a minute. He's in class right now." Val took another gulp of her smoothie. Her mother nodded her head at that before pushing herself up to her feet to finish getting ready for work. Once she had her bag and keys, she kissed her daughter on the forehead and whispered: "Be brave."

In the hour Val had left to kill she didn't feel particularly brave. She tried to be, to trick herself into it. She finished her smoothie and then went into her father's office. She opened up his top drawer and took out the envelope she had been avoiding.

The envelope then sat on the table in the living room for forty-two minutes. Val distracted herself with messaging Jennifer, who had also checked in recently although it was with a lot more messages involving witchcraft than Val would have liked. She also messaged James like she had told her mother she would, and the sight of his profile picture had her heart giving a feeble flip in her chest.

His response was instant. It was yet another offer to come over, with promises of food and snacks or whatever else she needed. That conversation burned up the remaining eighteen minutes and the knock at the door at precisely eleven AM shocked her enough for the phone to fumble from her fingers.

Val walked slowly to the door. She glanced behind her to look at Oz, but the German Shepard simply huffed through his nose as if he was telling her that she was on her own for this one.

Val's hand hovered over the doorknob. She could pretend she was napping. She could put this conversation off for another day. She could say she had developed agoraphobia specific to her room and then-

You're not going to leave my mother standing on the door-step, are you? An echo of Brock's voice whispered through the air. Val knew it was all in her head, but it still caused the ghost of a smile anyway. Her hand grasped the doorknob and she opened up the door to find that same smile on Mrs Walker's face.

Chapter Twenty

"I will never be able to thank you enough." Mrs Walker's hands were warm and clutched at Val's.

The pressure was the only thing that told Val she was in pain as well. Mrs Walker's makeup was flawless, her outfit well put together. She had even brought a gift bag with her. There were grapes and a container of homemade soup that she had placed in the kitchen. The bag wasn't empty, but the way Mrs Walker had clutched at it before placing it between her feet: it was something she wasn't sure she could part with.

"I didn't do anything." Val's throat felt scratchy from crying. She had explained to Mrs Walker everything that had happened at the hospital and as soon as she had started, she had found that she couldn't stop. She told Mrs Walker how Brock had been a hero and his unfinished business was something they could never have dreamed of; to save people from Logan Pierce.

Val had no doubt in her mind now that James would not have been spared. She would have hoped him running would have helped but if Logan got past Brock, Jess, and Val, it was unlikely that the only one to not see him would have made it out.

"You made him happy. You were his friend. You brought him back to me for that short little time." Mrs Walker listed her argument off on her fingers and Val shook her head.

"Brock did more for me than I ever did for him." Val insisted. "He was my best friend."

Mrs Walker gave Val's hand another squeeze at that, and she took a long deep breath. "I brought something else for you. A few things of his."

Mrs Walker reached for the bag and Val shook her head. "Mrs Walker, I really couldn't, please, I- "

"Need to stop calling me Mrs Walker," The middle-aged woman told her as she handed over the bright red gift bag. "Please. I want you to have them. He would want you to have them."

Val went to argue again. She had no right to these things, to Brock's things from when she wasn't even born. But the bag was in her hands and curiosity overrode the nauseous feeling in her stomach and so she reached into the bag.

Val pulled out Brock's letterman jacket and only realised she was crying when a tear hit the logo. "I can't take this from you. This must mean so much to your husband."

"He wants you to have it as well. Brock always joked he only went for the team for his dad and so his girl could wear his jacket. You're the closest thing he had to that." Mrs Walker reached out to gently stroke the arm. "I don't want it to stay in the closet anymore."

"Thank you so much." Val hugged the jacket to her chest. It had a faint smell to it, a mixture of a stale sharp cologne and baby powder. Val took in a deep breath through her nose and smiled slightly. "This is going to sound weird but- "

"But it smells like him. Fainter, much fainter, but it's like that smell was woven into the fabric." Mrs Walker nodded as she reached into the bag again.

Val had never known what Brock had smelt like. It was a weird question to ask Jess if she would have even known, and while Brock had once made a joke about smelling like sex appeal and champagne, it had never been a question at the forefront of her mind.

"This one is a little silly," Mrs Walker admitted, "and it's long since dead but...well we had whiteboards that we put around the house so Brock could talk to us. He wrote on them, about you and he mentioned that you loved them as well so..."

Val turned her attention towards the final item to come out of the bag and when she caught sight of what it was, she burst into watery laughter. The final item was a worn-out, baby blue original Furby.

Val took it gently in her hands, holding it between both of them like a precious stone as the jacket lay in her lap. "He always made fun of me for that." Val whispered. "Not seriously. He always knew when it was no longer a joke."

"He was always such a sassy child." Mrs Walker said.

"Oh, he never lost that. I think he just got more responsible."

"Well, they do say men only grow up at forty."

Both women laughed and the rest of the day passed much the same. Tears and laughter all mixed up together as they discussed Brock's habits and exchanged stories. There was a feeling in the room of no judgement. The two talked freely and cried just as much as each other. There was a sense of comfort, of understanding that they had both lost someone who meant the entire world to them.

As they hugged goodbye on the doorstep, Val promised that she would still come by the shop. Brock may be gone but she wasn't willing to let everything related to him slip away as well.

With that thought in mind, Val slipped her arms into the letterman jacket and curled herself up on the couch. Her eyes were sore, and her ankle was throbbing, but she finally felt that some of the crushing weight that had lodged itself between her heart and her lungs had been chipped away. It would never be gone just as Brock would never come back.

Val decided, however, that if that weight meant sure she never forgot Brock, then she would be happy to keep it. She didn't believe forgetting Brock would be possible even when she was old and grey. He was like James- a shooting star against an ink-black sky.

Val had given Mrs Walker the printed photos of Brock's final moments before moving on. It was the least that she could do, and Val had wished that James could have seen how happy they made her.

Val had not appreciated those photos enough, but now she picked up her phone and looked at them properly for the first time. In her favourite one, Brock and Val were both looking into the camera and smiling. Brock's grin was as bright as Val had ever seen it in print.

In the others, either Brock or Val was looking at the other while the other wasn't. Only one had them both looking at each other at the same time. Val wished that she could post them, show the world what it had just lost for the second time. Instead, she ordered for more to be printed online. She would put them up here like her mother thought she should.

She would also thank James for them. She hadn't done that yet. She was too concerned with wallowing in her grief and avoiding anything that made her happy to have even thought about it.

James made her happy, his text telling her he was on his way made her happy and rather than avoid the guilt that would follow that happiness, she would let it all wash over her.

Brock would have told her to sit up and stop crying over him although he was *so touched* that she was so upset over him. The thought of him up wherever he was looking down at her and grinning at the other 'angels' that all this was for him had Val softly laughing to herself.

Oz made a small whine at her and then trotted over to the door five seconds before there was a knock on it. Val was still smiling as she got up, her best friend's letterman jacket hanging off of her, and answered it.

James was stood there with messy black hair and a grey leather jacket. He paused for a second, a crooked smile on his face as he took in what she was wearing. Val reached up and ran her fingers across the embroidery that James was focusing on.

Brock Walker

James' eyes trailed up to her face. "It looks good on you."

Acknowledgements

Acknowledgements
In complete honesty, I'm not sure how to recognise everyone that helped this book come to be. The first thank you should go to you, the reader, for taking a chance on my little book. I hope you liked it.

There were the amazing American beta readers that helped keep me in line. As a Brit, some stuff just needed to be confirmed and verified even after research. The proof-readers that made sure all the slang and descriptions were also American (a lot of editing out the word sofa). Then there was the amazing cover designer that helped to show the funny romantic side of this ghost story perfectly.

Personal thanks go to Samantha Angus who stayed up until 2am reading only to message me that I made her cry, and that she would never forgive me. Spoiler alert- she has. I think. Your rants about Brock and Jess and James were invaluable, just like your friendship.

To my dad as well who once told me he thought I was going to be a writer when I grew up. Well...I'm fully grown now and every time I got writer's block or hit a plot hole I remember how confidently you told me that dad. It took me a few years, but I finally proved you right.

Finally, a big thank you to my partner Charlie. My soundboard, my number one supporter and maker of snacks. This book absolutely never would have been made without you. I would love to tell you that you have a character based on you, but the truth is they are all based on you. You are a part of every single character. You are Brock's morality, Jess's anger, Daniel's understanding. I love you.